CHECKMATE

Rita Y. Toews

CHECKMATE

DOUBLE DRAGON

CHAPTER ONE

Radvany, Hungary, 1941

He found mention of the war on page three of the Hungarian daily. Disheartened, Carl McCartney folded the slim newspaper and tossed it on the breakfast table. In England, news of Germany's march on Yugoslavia would have been the lead story of every Fleet Street publication. Here it was almost a footnote.

Since declaring itself neutral in 1939, Hungary continued to stick its head in the sand. Unbelievable naivety on the part of the county's leaders. At some point Hungary would be forced to deal with Hitler and Carl didn't want to be around when that day arrived.

Damn Don Maclean! And Philby as well.

Carl had come to Hungary on sabbatical to study Magyar history and languages, not to muck about in the shadow world of covert negotiations. The latest German advance made his continued stay in the chateau even more dangerous. He'd made a huge mistake when he'd agreed to act as a conduit for messages coming out of Eastern Europe. How the hell had he let himself be sucked in?

With or without instructions it was time to leave. But first, he'd have to do something with the last packet of correspondence and papers. The contents were explosive, and in the wrong hands he was pretty sure the English monarchy, and certain government leaders would be destroyed.

A burst of laughter intruded on his thoughts. Breakfast in the chateau's elegant, albeit chilly, dining room was coming to an end. Few of Count Karolyi's guests, the majority of whom were German, seemed concerned about events beyond the borders of the estate. Perhaps the unhindered advance of the German *blitzkrieg* made them cocksure, or, Carl mused, since they had paid to be treated like royalty they felt they were allowed royalty's disdain for anything that interfered with their personal pleasure.

Frau Schneider gave him a wave of acknowledgement and one of her looks that was far too intimate for Carl's taste, as she passed his table. A clutch of brightly dressed women followed in her wake. Their usual morning routine included several hours in the ladies lounge on the upper floor – strictly off-limits to the men, of course. Her husband joined the group of men gathering near the serving station. Plans were in the works for a boar hunt later in the day. Rows of anonymous Karolyi ancestors gazed down from portraits on the walls in stern approval of the men's aristocratic pastime.

Bela Makkos, the chateau's manager, caught Carl's eye. Makkos smiled as he approached Carl's table and addressed him in flawless English. "Professor McCartney, you have mail this morning." He laid a small pile of letters next to Carl's empty coffee cup. "I apologize once again for the carrier's late delivery, sir."

Like his employer, Count Karolyi, Makkos was a member of the aristocracy – although a minor one. In the past few decades much of Europe's nobility had fallen on hard times and now had to work for a living. If he resented his circumstances Makkos hid it well.

Carl fingered the bundle of letters, willing one to be from Don. God, this was such a mess! Last year's reunion at Cambridge to celebrate both Donald's upcoming nuptials and Carl's sabbatical had turned into a booze-soaked discussion of politics. A few too many gin and tonics, plus talk of down-trodden nations had resulted in an ill-conceived plan, and then Carl's commitment to 'assist in the cause of diplomacy'.

Discrete throat clearing drew Carl from his thoughts.

"Would you be interested in a game of chess this afternoon, Professor McCartney?" Makkos asked. Both Carl and the estate manager shared a passion for chess and had fallen into the routine of playing most afternoons. Unfortunately, Carl had lost respect for the man after inadvertently witnessing an incident between Makkos and a chamber maid, but he did enjoy the estate manager's skill as an opponent in chess. They were evenly matched, so the games had an intensity that allowed Carl to forget his circumstances for a short time.

He nodded in agreement. "I'd enjoy a game. Shall we say 3:00 o'clock, by the pool?"

Back in his room, he lit his second cigarette of the day as he sorted through the letters. Mail delivery had become quite unreliable. Often a glut of letters arrived followed by several weeks with no correspondence. He recognized his mother's handwriting, a letter from the research department. Yes ... Don! He tore the envelope open and removed the thin sheet of blue onion-skin paper. Amid general comments of life in France his friend cautioned, "If you have to leave Hungary quickly don't bother with your luggage, old chap. If it's time to get out, just leave it behind in storage. When things settle down you can always retrieve it."

Carl let the paper fall from his hands. Good God! What a cock-up. Had he wasted his time on all those daytrips? The so-called interviews that had nothing to do with his research? He retrieved the letter, tore it into small pieces and pulled the chain to flush it down the ancient loo. If it hadn't been for the documents and notes he would have been out of Hungary weeks ago. Now the German army was advancing on one side and the Russians on the other. In chess terms, Hungary was the pawn in an opening gambit.

Carl pulled his straw hat lower over his brow to ward off the sun's rays. If it was this hot in June, what would it be like in August? The heat, and his dilemma over the documents made concentrating on the chess game doubly difficult.

His wandering gaze settled on a distraction in the pool. An insect had fallen into the water. The tiny creature's struggles sent small water ripples fanning outward in ever-growing concentric circles. Below the surface the black and white tiles on the bottom of the pool resembled the chess board in front of him. The war, life-- it was all like a chess game. A deadly serious one, but a game all the same. Every move and countermove had consequences across the board.

Makkos offered up a King's Bishop's Pawn.

As Carl reached for a knight, the afternoon's outward appearance of tranquillity shattered when a young serving girl rushed from the chateau in tears. "Kassa was bombed! By the Russians! Kassa was bombed!"

Kassa, a not insignificant city about fifty kilometres from where they sat. Carl's stomach knotted. Hungary would now be forced into her opening move. It was time to "store the luggage" and leave by any means possible.

CHAPTER TWO

Budapest – Today

Stan placed a protective arm around Sonja's shoulders as he steered her past a group of British tourists gathered around their tour guide. His wife glanced up to smile her thanks and a wave of warmth spread south from his gut. They'd been married for six months and one look from her could still turn him on. He raised an eyebrow in return and added a lecherous grin.

"Stan! Behave yourself." Feigned shock permeated her tone. "I'm supposed to be giving you a tour of Budapest."

"But, we're on our honeymoon." To the delighted whistles and claps of bystanders, he swept her into his arms and kissed her. The members of his RCMP detachment back in Winnipeg would be shocked by their superior's public display of affection. In truth, more than one would be envious, given the charms and beauty of the woman in his arms.

Sonja disengaged herself with a laugh and pushed her dark hair back into place. "Honeymoon or not, we're going to see the sites today. Now listen. That beautiful palace across the river...."

Stan struggled to pay attention. It was a relief to see her so carefree. He had initially questioned her suggestion to visit Hungary for their honeymoon. Why would she want to return to the place where her dreams, and her body, had been sold to the highest bidder? He suspected it had less to do with confronting her past than it had with finding her miserable excuse for a brother.

"Perhaps to look for Ferenc," she admitted when Stan

probed. Whenever she was stressed Sonja slipped back into the heavy Ukrainian accent she had worked so hard to soften. "He is my only family now. We can just look for him, yes?"

Stan wasn't sure how he would react if they did find Ferenc. How a brother could smuggle his beautiful desperate sister out of Ukraine into Hungary, then use her to pay down a drug debt, was beyond Stan's understanding. As a member of the Royal Canadian Mounted Police he had often gone undercover to infiltrate drug organizations, so he was familiar with the darker side of people's nature. Still, he had never expected he would have a brother-in-law who fell into that category. As far as Stan was concerned Feri, as Sonja often referred to him, could stay missing.

His thoughts were interrupted when he realized his wife stood, arms crossed, waiting for him to notice she no longer played tour guide. Her hazel-green eyes narrowed with mock annoyance. "Stan! You aren't paying attention to what I'm saying." She softened. "Have you had enough?"

He smiled and shook his head, then pushed the troubling thoughts aside as he focussed on the Royal Palace that dominated the opposite shore of the Danube. Serving as a backdrop, Buda's forested hills glowed with September colour in a palette ranging from bright yellow to deep violet. A cloudless blue sky completed the setting. Impressive. It reminded him of fall in the hills near Gatineau, Quebec.

"During the Second World War the palace was one of the last areas of resistance against Russia's Red Army. It was totally destroyed just months before the war ended and then rebuilt..." Sonja lowered her guidebook. "Europe has such a violent past compared to Canada."

10

"Its present is still pretty grim," Stan replied. "Organized crime, terrorist groups, drug trafficking, nuclear weapons sales...." He left out the obvious additional activity but Sonja caught the omission. The excitement in her eyes died.

"And exporting young girls to North America for the sex trade."

"Sonja, I'm sorry. I wasn't thinking."

"Come," she said as she jammed the guidebook and her camera in her purse. "We'll go have a refreshment and forget about crime for a while. Your job should have stayed at home."

Stan swore under his breath. Their chances of locating Feri were practically nil, yet found or unfound, the bastard was messing with their honeymoon.

They strolled along the promenade in the direction of Vaci utca, Budapest's version of New York's Fifth Avenue. When he took her hand in his and gave it a gentle squeeze she smiled in acknowledgement. *I'm a lucky man*, Stan reflected.

Tourists, responding to the lure of the balmy afternoon temperature, were out in droves. A smattering of Ukrainian and, not infrequently, English, fell on his ear from those passing by. It gave his spirits a lift to know there were people around he could talk to, and understand, if need be. In the rural areas they'd passed through on their way to Budapest he often had to rely on Sonja as his interpreter.

The Vaci utca was off limits to cars so pedestrians filled the street. Ornate shops, their windows crammed with merchandise from across Hungary as well as Europe, did their best to tempt shoppers to part with their money. He leaned against an ornamented lamppost, one eye on the crowd, the other on his wife as she examined first a

11

display of pottery, and then a table of embroidery and intricate lacework.

Two boys on skateboards, the wheels chattering on the paving stones, caught his attention when they were still a half block away. They were expert, perhaps too expert. Stan's muscles tensed as the boys wove their way around the kiosks and outdoor display tables narrowly missing Sonja when they shot by. The cop in him wanted to caution her to put the strap of her purse over her head to the opposite shoulder rather than clutching it under her arm, but he forced the thought aside. As she'd said, the cop should have stayed at home.

Her interest in the display satisfied, Sonja moved to rejoin him but stopped to allow a couple pushing a pram to pass. Her face brightened at the sight of a drooling baby. When she shot him a glance, Stan's stomach did a flip. Children? He was pushing thirty so there was nothing wrong with the timing. Still... The image of a toddler, a copy of himself with the same dark hair and brown eyes, sprang to mind. How did men learn to be fathers? Yet *another* conversation he wished he could have with his own father. He shook his head; questions this big called for a glass of wine.

With a firm grip on his wife's elbow, he directed her toward an attractive restaurant with tables that spilled onto the sidewalk. A soft Strauss melody and the aroma of chocolate surrounded them as the waiter led them to a bistro table set for two. "Here. Practise your Hungarian." Sonja handed him a leather-bound wine list.

He groaned aloud as she rewarded him with another smile. He could speak French, English and Ukrainian. Why was Hungarian such a struggle? He'd even taken a course before they left Canada but the Magyar language with its fourteen vowels still eluded him. His roaming finger came to rest on an entry near the top of the list. "How about *Egri Bikavér*?

"Bull's blood," translated Sonja. At the startled look on his face she broke into a laugh. "No, no. You said it right, but that's what it means. Bull's blood. It's really quite a famous red wine from --"

Her words ended in a harsh gasp. Something on the street behind him had caught her attention. Something that drained the colour from her face.

Stan twisted in his seat to follow her line of vision. A small group made their way along the street - several stylishly dressed women escorted by a dark-haired man in his late forties. He was tall, dressed in a two-piece suit that could never have come off the rack. A dusky complexion coupled with a thin black moustache that traced a line above full lips spoke of Latino, or Gypsy, heritage. At first glance, he seemed an elegant gentleman. It was when Stan sought his eyes that the illusion shattered - they were the wary eyes of a predator.

"Sipos. Sipos Sandor." Sonja spoke the name so softly Stan thought he had misunderstood. What were the chances they'd run into Sipos on their second day in Budapest?

***

Sonja leaned over the sink and splashed more cold water on her face. Her nausea had lessened. She had put Sipos so firmly out of her mind that it never occurred to her she might see him in Budapest. A shiver crawled up her spine and she shook her shoulders in a small dance to drive it away. She wouldn't let him ruin her honeymoon - or her new life. She wasn't the same innocent girl she had been two years ago. She had someone who loved her, and

13

she had learned how to defend herself. In fact, she'd learned that lesson so well she had almost killed a man.

She dried her face and ran a comb through her hair. Even if she didn't feel like eating, Stan must be hungry by now. They could find a little restaurant and decide if they should leave Budapest. Maybe they could drive to Lake Balaton, or go north to the wine region. She had been foolish to think she could find her brother here after all this time.

The ring of the phone in the suite's main room ended abruptly. Stan voice, the words indistinct, reached her through the closed door. Odd. Only a few people knew where they were.

CHAPTER THREE

Yesterday's pleasant weather had given way overnight to lower temperatures and a steady drizzle. As the taxi passed through the garden district of Buda en route to the Canadian embassy, Stan wiped condensation from the window to get a better view of the villas and mansions on either side of the street.

He'd certainly had a misconception of Hungary. This was no backward country stuck in the dark ages, especially Budapest. Hungary had once been a dynamic, prosperous nation. Sadly, quick glimpses of the magnificent houses they passed told a story of decades-long neglect. No wonder the Hungarians felt no love for the Soviets. Since the Second World War when the Communists gained control they had used their iron rule to rape and reduce the nation to destitution.

A woman walking with her dog on the sidewalk stepped back to avoid a spray of water from the cab's passage. Given the miserable weather, Stan was glad Sonja had decided to stay at the hotel. After the shock of seeing Sipos Sandor yesterday, she suggested they leave the capital. Stan agreed. Budapest, for all its history and beauty, had lost its appeal with that single glimpse of the man. There were other regions of Hungary that had a lot to offer tourists. Once they were away from the capital he would do whatever it took to bring back the sense of adventure and light mood that had marked the start of their holiday.

While Stan visited the embassy Sonja said she would collect maps of the outlying districts and chart a route for the remainder of their stay. And, she hadn't given up on finding Feri. She wanted to give it one last shot. He had no Facebook or other internet presence, but there was still the phone book to check. Perhaps there was a phone number listed for him. If not, she wanted to visit the address she remembered from two years earlier, although she agreed there was little chance he was still there. Stan was confident Sonja was on a wild goose chase so he was sure they would be able to leave Budapest by late afternoon.

A stunning three-story villa on a small rise caught his eye. When he saw the Canadian flag flying inside the gate a feeling of pride ran through him. The taxi pulled into the circular driveway. "Canadian embassy, sir," the driver stated. Farther down the slope an ugly cube-shaped building appeared to be the centre of some activity. The driver noted Stan's interest and explained, "Visa office, passport, such things. One day I stand there for passport, then go to Canada." His accent was heavy but the meaning was clear.

The car pulled to a stop at an armed barrier. After confirming his name was on a list of expected visitors, Stan paid the driver, raised the hood on his jacket against the rain, and picked his way around the puddles pockmarking the cobbled courtyard.

The phone call from the embassy the previous afternoon had come as a surprise. The secretary offered no information but requested Stan meet with the ambassador at 8:30 the following morning.

Stan considered the possibilities. Their passports and paperwork should be in order. If there was a problem with their flights the airlines would take care of that, and they hadn't broken any laws he was aware of. The only reason that made sense didn't sit well with him--the request to visit might be work-related. Only a national emergency would tempt him to cancel this holiday.

The scent of beeswax rubbed into rich wood over decades greeted him as he entered the embassy's outer foyer. He stopped, closed his eyes and drew a deep breath. Memories of attending mass with his parents at St. Boniface Cathedral in Winnipeg flooded back from his childhood.

Beeswax, old wood, incense... He had found the hushed, dim interior of the huge cathedral and the symbolism of the mass comforting when he was young but even so, both he and his father stopped going after his mother's death. The mysteries and promises of the religious ceremony could not fill the emptiness of the space she had occupied beside them on the pew.

In the foyer a guard checked his identification before pointing him in the direction of the ambassador's reception area. He stripped off his wet jacket as he approached the desk. "Stan Boyko," he announced to the young woman sitting there. A nameplate identified her as 'Louise Craddock' a name, Stan thought, more suited to a woman several decades older than the twenty-something receptionist eyeing him with apprehension.

Fingers with nails bitten to the quick tapped information on the computer keys.

"Would that be Constable Stanley Boyko and Mrs. Sonja Boyko?" She glanced behind Stan as though looking for another person.

"Partially correct, Louise. You can make that Corporal--."

"Oh, no, I... I'm not Louise." A flush crept up her neck to stain her cheeks.

When Stan glanced at the nameplate she reached for it and tucked it in a drawer. "Louise was in an accident two days ago and I'm--" Her hands flew to her mouth. "Oh, my God. I probably shouldn't have said that. We're

17

not supposed to give out any personal information. Oh, brother." The remains of a nail succumbed to sharp teeth.

Overwhelmed and under-trained in the position, Stan decided. Probably the only woman in the typing pool with enough Hungarian to replace the injured Louise. Best to make light of it.

"Then we have something in common. I've also received a new position. You can change your records to read Corporal Stan Boyko. Mrs. Boyko didn't come with me this morning."

The flustered receptionist made several attempts to work her magic with the computer keys. The effort with an unfamiliar system resulted in a series of beeps.

"Miss?"

She glanced up, eyes bright with gathering tears.

"I'll just take a seat here in the waiting room. That will give you a chance to make the changes without me hanging over the desk. Will the wait be long?"

"Oh, no, not long. I'll just, ...I'll just finish this and bring you a coffee, okay?"

Thick Turkish carpets centred on marble floors muffled his footsteps as he circled the spacious room. Heavy draperies swathed mullioned windows fitted with bevelled glass. A sofa and two club chairs set at right angles to the marble-faced fireplace tempted him to run his hand over the buttery softness of the high-end leather. Overall, an impressive waiting room. One of the best he'd encountered. Canada had done very well for itself in the Hungarian capital.

As he settled into the embrace of one of the club chairs a stack of magazines on the coffee table caught his attention. He considered, then chose one at random. Although he wasn't in a great hurry, he hoped the young woman would remember to advise the ambassador he was waiting.

The magazine proved current, and written in English, although it contained only Hungarian news items. One story immediately caught his eye: **Canada Safe Haven or Immigration Scheme**

Hungarian immigration scheme...he'd seen something about this back home. Right! A few days before he'd left Canada there had been a report out of Ottawa from CSIS mentioning a Gypsy scam. The details of the report proved elusive, flirting on the edge of his memory, but staying just out of reach. He thumbed through the magazine looking for the article.

When he found it a quick read jogged his memory. An immigration scam used so successfully in the Czech Republic several years earlier was now being used in Hungary. For a hefty fee Gypsies, desperate for jobs and decent schooling for their children, were promised easy entry into Canada if they claimed persecution in Hungary. They were told that once in Canada, they were guaranteed acceptance as refugees and given jobs and free housing. Dozens of families had already borrowed heavily and sold everything they owned to raise the price of the illegal documentation package with instructions and carefully worded storylines.

Stan shook his head in wonder. How could anyone prey on people already so desperate? When it came to taking advantage of the less fortunate, mankind could be very disingenuous. Sipos Sandor came to mind along with an image of the pain on Sonja's beautiful face. Stan clamped a lid on the thought and turned his attention back to the magazine.

The article's author, Allan Howland, an American correspondent living in Hungary, went on to say that the Hungarian government was investigating several leads in

19

their bid to end the illegal scheme. From experience Stan knew the words meant little to desperate people.

Instinct honed over years of undercover work warned him he was being watched. As he glanced up the receptionist returned the phone to its cradle and nodded in his direction. "Ambassador Graham will see you now, Mr. Boyko."

CHAPTER FOUR

The ambassador's office was impressive, much like the waiting room. Stan noted a seating area with comfortable chairs off to one side, but it was the formal work area with its large desk that dominated the room. Canadian and Hungarian flags flanked a large window offering an impressive view of the Buda hills. Other than a painting of an east-coast fishing village on one wall, and a family photo on the credenza, there was little to reveal the nature of the man behind the desk.

"Corporal Boyko, I must apologize for interrupting your holiday." Ambassador Graham, a slim man whose sparse salt and pepper hair sprang from his head like a nimbus, left his desk to extend a hand in greeting.

The grip was brief but firm; a sign of a man who would be concise but who would pay attention to details. There would be no time spent on chit-chat when there was business to accomplish. Stan wondered what toll the flustered receptionist had on someone who appreciated order and efficiency. For both their sakes, he hoped her assignment was short-lived.

"I admit I'm surprised and curious," Stan acknowledged as he followed the Ambassador's lead and settled into a chair facing the desk. "We haven't run afoul of any laws during our wanderings, have we?" They had started their holiday with a few days in Vienna, then rented a car and toured the western portion of Hungary as they worked their way to Budapest.

"No, no. Nothing like that." Graham gave his head an emphatic shake, like a terrier shaking its prey. "But, I'll be the first to admit this meeting is extremely unusual." He eyed Stan for a moment, leaving the impression he was weighing his options on how to continue. "I received a call from Ottawa yesterday asking me to use my capacity here to act as a messenger. And before you leave the embassy today, you're asked to contact Inspector Willis at 'D' Division. I believe that's in Winnipeg?"

Shit. This summons *was* work-related. He had a month of holidays coming to him and he would use every day of it. He'd make that clear when he made the call to Mark. "It is. Inspector Mark Willis is my superior."

The ambassador acknowledged the comment with a nod. "A situation of some delicacy has surfaced." His bottom lip shot out a fraction then retreated, "I suppose there are some in government circles who would characterize it as a potential for scandal while others would laugh at the banality of it all. Either way, the matter has implications for the monarchy...eh, well maybe more for the Brits as a whole. As a member of the Commonwealth, Canada is being asked to do a bit of digging on behalf of the British government."

"A scandal concerning the British? If there's a problem for the Crown why aren't the British investigating it themselves?"

"Fair question. And one I posed myself. But as I said, it involves the monarchy to a certain extent but it goes much farther than that. It seems MI-5 have concerns if they try to deal with it internally. Their Freedom of Information Act gave so much power to the British press that informants have popped up in all governmental agencies, including MI-5. And since this situation is not a security risk which would give it a high classification, there's a pretty good chance word of the investigation would leak if they handle it. Still, if I...." His fingers beat a brief tattoo on the arm of the chair. "Well, whatever you or I might think, they've asked Canada for help."

Stan's mind raced. What the hell? Work with MI5? Did his superiors want him to become an agent?

"Your reputation as an investigator has come to the attention of certain individuals in official circles, Corporal Boyko. And since you're already in Hungary, Ottawa has asked if you would go on loan to the British government."

Silence hung in the air as Stan tried to collect his thoughts. One moment he was a man on vacation with his wife, the next he was being asked to investigate a sensitive issue on behalf of another country. Outside a car horn sounded. Someone was impatient, ready to get on with their day. As was he. Stan leaned forward in the chair. He'd put an end to this business right now.

"Sorry, but someone's got the wrong information. I'm not here in an official capacity. My wife and I are on our honeymoon. We'll spend a bit more time in Hungary and then we're off to the Greek islands for a few weeks to soak up the sun."

Graham cleared his throat. "They realize you're on your honeymoon...and that it's an inconvenience."

Stan caught the gravity in the comment. Somewhere up the food chain someone had put pressure on the man. Now that pressure was being transferred to him.

The ambassador steepled his fingers. "Ottawa feels you're in a unique position. You have the qualifications they need, you're already on location, and you have the acceptable security clearance."

"The qualifications they need? That's a joke. I can't even speak Hungarian. I'm sorry," he rose to leave, "but they'll have to get someone else. Better yet, let MI-5 deal with their own problems." He chuckled to relieve the tension. "They can put their legendary James Bond on it."

"I'm told your wife is fluent in Hungarian."

It was a simple statement, but it said much. Whatever agency pulled the strings had already considered his lack of language skills and was willing for Sonja to act as his interpreter. To allow civilian involvement meant the investigation was deemed a very low risk. Interesting. At least he could listen to what the proposal was.

Stan sat. "Anything more you can tell me about this sensitive matter?"

"Nothing too onerous would be required, but as you said, it is sensitive. I'm told it will be possible to do the investigation while you and your wife tour Hungary."

"And I suppose I'll be thoroughly briefed only when I've accepted the job?"

Graham smiled but did not reply.

Stan sorted through his options. There could be repercussions for saying yes as well as for saying no. Officers who turned down assignments found their opportunities for advancement restricted. Accepting may or may not cut into his vacation, but at least they wouldn't have to leave Hungary. And given the circumstances, he would probably be compensated with additional time off, plus expenses. That alone made the request attractive. Extra time to relax in Greece with Sonja appealed to him.

A small voice of caution nagged in the back of his mind. Gone were his bachelor days when decisions could be made without considering someone else. He didn't have the right to involve Sonja in an investigation, no matter how low the risk, without her consent. Still, Sonja had always shown a keen interest in his work and had proven in the past that she could keep her head in tense situations. He was reasonably confident she would find the situation an exciting addition to their vacation. And, it would take her mind off both Sipos and Feri.

"Well, Ambassador Graham, given what you've said, you can tell the British they have a new agent."

CHAPTER FIVE

Stan left the embassy and hailed a cab. Facts, questions and hastily conceived ideas careened through his thoughts. Sonja would have a field day with the information. When he accepted the assignment he thought it would involve nothing more than a few interviews to collect information. In reality, it was a treasure hunt for lost documents. A very intriguing treasure hunt that could cause some degree of embarrassment to the British government. The politics of the country were divided already so he could see problems if agitators got their hands on the documents.

As the driver guided the taxi through the noon-hour press of traffic Stan thought back over the briefing.

***

A light tap on the office door and fumbling of the handle halted their conversation and brought Ambassador Graham to his feet. The receptionist entered balancing a tray with coffee, mugs, cream and sugar. "You've met Jordan?" the ambassador asked. "She's filling in for a few weeks."

Stan acknowledged the young lady with a smile as she arranged the coffee items on the desk. When she turned to leave she glanced at him and stated, proudly: "You'll be glad to know the coffee is Canada's own Tim Horton's."

The ambassador's forehead furrowed as he watched her leave. Whether in concern or annoyance Stan could not tell. The moment was short-lived. The older man spooned sugar into his cup then lead into the briefing.

"During the first two years of the Second World War Hungary remained a neutral nation. She kept her distance from the countries determined to annihilate each other and those threatening to join in. Unfortunately, that neutrality created the perfect milieu for espionage and intelligence activities within her borders. Hungary was the natural link between Germany and the Soviets. Operatives from both countries were everywhere. Britain, of course, had her own eyes and ears strategically placed to gather information vital to her war efforts. Are you aware of a nasty little group called the Cambridge spy ring?"

Stan took another sip of coffee before answering. It was delicious. A taste of home. "Vaguely. Communist sympathizers infiltrated British intelligence. A few names that come to mind are Maclean, Blunt and maybe ... a fellow named Philby? That's right. I believe Philby lead the ring."

"So it seemed at the time. Recently the Soviets have opened their archives and it turns out it was Anthony Blunt who led the ring. Blunt was a distant cousin of the Queen and she had entrusted him with the supervision of her art collection. That gave him ready access to the royal family, including the Duke of Windsor. Blunt also served in MI-5." He studied Stan over the rim of his cup. "His job was to keep the neutral missions located in London-- including Hungary's--under surveillance. And to make matters worse, he also sat on the Joint Intelligence Committee, so he had access to material from the code breakers at Bletchley Park."

A low whistle escaped Stan's pursed lips. "That's like a fox loose in a henhouse."

"The story only gets worse, I'm afraid. In 1941, Maclean recruited a Cambridge lecturer of English literature by the name of Carl McCartney into the group.

McCartney was a writer about to leave for Hungary on sabbatical, supposedly to do research for his next book."

Stan nodded. "The perfect cover."

Graham agreed. "According to a Soviet source, McCartney was the conduit for secret negotiations between Hitler's emissary, Rudolph Hess, and the Duke of Windsor. Hitler had proposed an alliance with Britain against Russia. Speculation is that the correspondence would have gone through McCartney, to Maclean, to Blunt and from Blunt to the Duke. "

Stan held up a hand. "Hold it a minute. It's old news that the Duke of Windsor had a friendly relationship with Hitler."

"Rumours are one thing, they can be dismissed. For example, when Hess implied that the Duke was invited to negotiate an alliance between the Reich and the British Empire, Britain denied his statement. And the written documentation in the famous Windsor File was dismissed by the queen as evidence of what the Germans were *trying* to do, and of how completely they failed. But apparently, as most things are, the reality wasn't that cut and dried.

With the help of the Duke of Coburg secret negotiations were being conducted in 1940 to form a new English government with the Duke of Windsor at the helm. The plan was that Britain would make peace with Germany, forming a military alliance against the USSR. It seems there are documents, even photographs, which prove it.

"The British people are a bit disenchanted with their government these days. There's open resentment for the wars in Iraq and Afghanistan. Add to that the business of Brexit ..." Graham spread his hands in resignation. "The contents of those documents could be added fodder in the

28

hands of groups trying to spread even more anger against the government." Graham paused and considered Stan before continuing.

"There's more. And this is the part that might really be sticking in the British government's craw since, as you say, the Duke of Windsor and his sympathy for Hitler is pretty much "old news".

Topping up his coffee, Stan nodded for the ambassador to continue as he reached for cream.

"Given your age," Graham raised an eyebrow and smiled, "you'll need a bit of background on the main player in this "alleged" conspiracy. Earlier in his career Winston Churchill, Britain's wartime leader, was an unabashed admirer of Mussolini and fascism."

The cream jug on its way to the mug halted as Stan shot the Ambassador a look. "You're kidding me, right."

"No. That view changed in the late '30s but rumours circulated in 1940 that Churchill was in direct correspondence on three occasions with Mussolini."

"Why on earth...?" Stan abandoned the coffee to concentrate on what Ambassador Graham was saying.

"Mhmm... pretty explosive stuff." Graham granted. "Reports state he asked, or begged, depending on who the narrator is, that "Il Duce" promise Italy would stay neutral, and that he would intercede with Hitler to grant peace terms that would not affect Britain's independence."

"What made him think Mussolini would agree to anything like that?"

"Oh, the "quid pro quo" was pretty sweet. He offered them Malta in exchange. One can only imagine what the Maltese would have thought of that arrangement. Apparently France was willing to throw in a few scattered islands in the Mediterranean but Malta was the prize that would tempt Mussolini."

Stan sat back to review what he'd just been told. The sound of a lawnmower on the embassy grounds, formerly white noise, registered in his sub-conscience and brought him back to the present. "Do the British know where the papers are? Who has them?"

"No. That's the problem. McCartney managed to make it back to England when all hell broke loose on the continent. He died, of natural causes I might add, in 1978. He always denied any involvement in gathering the information and none of his supposed henchmen ever implicated him. It was only after his death that confirmation could be made through his private papers.

"The British always assumed the Russians had the documents, but no copies turned up when the Russian opened the archives. Unfortunately, the interest they showed while searching the archives stirred curiosity and now both countries are eager to get their hands on whatever it is that's out there. The British would be most grateful if they are found and turned over to them."

"So this isn't a James Bond scenario with dire consequences if the mission fails?"

Graham grimaced. "Not really, but... Well, there's always been a fair number of Brits who have nothing good to say about Churchill. These papers would only add fuel to the fire. Something the government wants to avoid at all costs."

From what he now knew, Stan agreed. "Why do they think the papers are still here in Hungary? McCartney could have passed them on to his friends after he returned to England."

"It's not supported by what the investigation found at the time. It's more likely Carl McCartney hid the papers when he fled Hungary in 1941. While here, the professor was a paying guest in a hunting lodge on the estate of Count Karolyi, near a place called Radvany."

"A *paying* guest? That sounds like a contradiction to me."

The ambassador smiled. "A nice way of saving face for a prestigious family who had fallen on hard times. In reality, their hunting lodge had been turned into a hotel for anyone with the money to pay. How a Cambridge professor had that much disposable income is also a mystery. One that would be explained if someone else was footing the bill."

Stan's task had just become more difficult. If the lodge was, in fact, a hotel that meant other guests were there at the time. How many other guests, and how many had been like McCartney - the eyes and ears of a spy organization?

"Is the lodge still used as a hotel today?" Maybe he and Sonja could check in and nose around a little. The hunting lodge of a Count couldn't be too shabby, and it might make up for combining work with their vacation. A ripple of pleasure passed through him. The trail was over seventy years old. Sonja would be in no danger, and knowing his wife, she would relish the challenge of the hunt.

"Afraid not. The place was abandoned during the war and pretty much went to ruin. The Count's employees, those who are still alive, came from the village of Radvany, only a kilometre or two away. I know it's not much to go on but it's all we have."

"I'll need a cover story, a reason for asking questions in the area."

"Of course. Just give me a moment." Graham sorted through several files on his desk before removing one from a stack. "I kept Jordan quite late last night working on the necessary documentation."

After extracting a document he retrieved a packet from the desk and relocked the drawer. "We've had a bit of a problem lately with a group preying on Gypsies. Three families and a single man have asked for refugee status in Canada."

"I was just reading about that in the waiting room. They claim they were persecuted by the Hungarian authorities."

Graham nodded. "Of course the authorities deny it." He handed some of the papers to Stan. "One of the individuals comes from Szephalom, another village near the chateau. You can say you've been sent to investigate his refugee claim. The authorities there say he murdered a man. He says they're trying to pin something on him to get it off their books." Graham also handed Stan an envelope. "There's an advance in there for expenses. Spend it wisely." He smiled at his small joke.

"Is there information on Carl McCartney in the documents? Anything that will give me some insight into the man?" He set the now cold cup of coffee back on the desk.

"There's not much to go on, I'm afraid. He was a very private individual. Not surprising, given his activities. His school records indicate he was an avid chess player and belonged to several groups. I don't suppose that will be of much help to you, though."

With that, he handed Stan a pen and indicated where he should sign the paperwork that would finalize his appointment.

***

The taxi drew up to the hotel. It was time to tell

32

Sonja the honeymoon was over, and why.

CHAPTER SIX

Sonja's mood had brightened when he related his conversation with the ambassador. "Really, Stan? How interesting! We'll be like spies?"

"Well, in a way I suppose, but not really," he cautioned as he packed his suitcase and made a final tour of the room for any forgotten items. "I guess you could say we'll be compensated for doing a bit of nosing around. I don't think it will amount to much. It's too bad the chateau isn't being used. It would have made the search less difficult."

She packed the last of her items in her suitcase before replacing the phone book in the desk. "There is no phone listed for Feri. We will have to go to the apartment."

His heart sank. Returning to the neighbourhood would bring the memories that much closer.

***

Stan pulled the rental car to the curb at 324 Lehel utca, the address where Sonja had spent her final days with Feri before leaving for Canada. Neither he nor Sonja spoke much on the trip from the hotel.

Other than brief directions: "left here", "I think...this way", Sonja appeared lost in thought. Stan realized the prospect of coming face to face with the person who sold you into the sex trade would be daunting for anyone, more so when that person was your brother.

As they sat at the curb he watched in silent sympathy as she struggled to reach a decision--should she get out of the car or ask him to drive on. He would prefer the latter but the decision was not his to make.

He reached over and stroked her cheek with the edge of a finger. "You don't have to do this, sweetheart. We can just point the car out of town and drive. You can leave it all behind you."

The early morning rain clouds had been bullied over the horizon by a high-pressure system from the north. As well as bringing sunshine, it carried the promise of much cooler days for Budapest. A shaft of weak sunlight illuminated her features as she turned to look at him.

"That would not be so easy for me. I have you, yes, but no other family. I need to know what happened to him. He was so sick when I left. Perhaps if he is still alive there is something I can do for him. Some way I can help him." She swallowed hard then turned her gaze through the car window to the apartment beyond. "Some things in a family, maybe they must be confronted and forgiven before they can be--as you say -- 'left behind.'" She brightened as a thought hit her. "And besides, it is because of him that I went to Canada and we found each other."

Her decision made, Sonja opened the car door and stepped to the curb. Behind her, she heard Stan lock the car, then move to her side. His presence was a comfort. Each step closer to the familiar building weakened her resolve. Feri had destroyed her life once, if she let him in again he might jeopardize the new life she had found with Stan.

As a girl she never dreamt that the happiness she knew now could be possible. Growing up in Ukraine had been a soul-numbing experience for her. No, she reflected, not just her -- for her entire family. Their father disappeared while she was still a young girl, swept up as a political dissident during one of the government's regular

35

purges. When their mother retreated into herself, finding solace in religion, Feri became the only stable point in Sonja's life. Her rock, her hero.

Then one night, shortly after his twentieth birthday, Feri disappeared. He'd found a way to cross the border into Hungary to start a new life. In his farewell note, he promised he would establish himself and send for her. They would live in freedom together and find the happiness that had eluded them in Ukraine.

It was only after their mother's death that he managed to smuggle her into Hungary, but the same illegal connections that helped him with her transport had the ultimate hold on him. Feri was a small-time player in a high-stakes game and he had slipped up. He began to sample his supplier's product. His offering to make up the shortfall and appease his boss, Sipos Sandor? His beautiful but naive sister, Sonja.

For months after she arrived in Hungary she had refused Sipos' requests to appear in his movies or act as an escort for wealthy men. Sonja brushed tears from her eyes as she remembered the day Feri brought her to meet his boss for the final confrontation. Sipos made it clear Feri's debt would have to be paid, one way or another.

"I'm a reasonable man, Sonja." He nodded to her brother who cowered behind her in a chair. "Just ask Feri. If one of my employees is unhappy with our working arrangement I do my best to find a solution that suits us both. In your case, my dear," his eyes travelled across her body, "since you don't seem agreeable to employment with me, I have an alternate proposal for you."

His proposal was to introduce her to a Canadian woman travelling through Hungary recruiting girls for her business. If Rosa Sinclair found Sonja suitable, Sipos

36

would receive a finder's fee that would be sufficient to discharge Feri's debt. One look at her brother's face told Sonja the nature of the Canadian business.

But it hadn't been all bad, Sonja reminded herself as she reached for Stan's hand. In Canada, the police were watching Rosa. In the end, Stan had exposed the whole sorry mess before Rosa could force Sonja to work in her "escort service". Her saviour had later become her husband.

She glanced at Stan, found comfort in the warmth of his smile, and closed the distance to the apartment's entrance. *To move forward I must rid the ghosts of the past.*

There was no F. Sepsik listed on the mutilated directory panel beside the glass entrance door. Not surprising really, Stan thought. Two years can bring a lot of changes for a man on drugs.

Sonja squared her shoulders and pressed the buzzer labelled "manager". After a few sentences of unintelligible garble, the intercom went dead. While Sonja paced the cracked sidewalk Stan stared through the door at a small lobby that replicated many he had passed through while working undercover in Canada. Tattered announcements plastered a bulletin board near the single elevator door. Stuffed into a corner, beside a row of battered letterboxes, a yellowing corn plant struggled to survive. No sense of welcome or refuge greeted the tenants who passed through these doors on their way to the four cinder-block walls that comprised their apartment. Most would be as desperate as Ferenc Sepsik.

Several minutes passed before a woman lumbered down the hallway. She pushed through the door but kept a slippered foot in place to hold it open.

As Stan watched the exchange between his wife and

the landlady he knew it wasn't going well. Sonja touched his elbow at one point, then dropped her hand to her shoulder bag and gripped it tightly. The landlady crossed her beefy arms, drew a deep breath into her impressive lungs and clammed up. Sonja turned to offer an explanation. "She remembers him, but he left last year. She said she doesn't know where he went, but she did see him again a few months ago in a *csemege*. That is how you say a deli in Hungarian. She wants to know what it is worth to me to have this information."

Without waiting for advice Sonja addressed the woman again. After a few more sentences the landlady planted one hand on her hip and the other on the door jamb as she stood her ground.

Once again Sonja explained. "He always paid his rent, and he looked well when he left but she says she will not tell me more unless I pay."

"Offer her 4,000 forints for the shop's name and address." When he reached for his wallet the landlady's heavy face split into a smile.

CHAPTER SEVEN

Panna Sepsik scooped the toddler from the floor and gently disengaged the fragile figurine from the child's hand. "No, no, Eva, you mustn't touch." She smothered the child's face with kisses to stop the wailing and carried her to the back room of the shop.

Feri glanced up from the open packing crate that he just arrived and smiled as his wife approached with the angry child. Reaching over, he chucked Eva under the chin. "Hey now. It's not that bad." Eva gulped and extended her chubby arms to her father.

"Really, Feri, you spoil her," Panna chided as she surrendered the girl.

"How can I not? She's the spitting image of her mother. Her eyes, her hair, both black as coal. And see, she already has a beautiful bloom on her cheeks. Like you, she will need no make-up when she grows older."

Panna laughed as she gathered her mass of black curls together and secured them with an elastic band at the nape of her neck. "That bloom on her cheeks means she's teething, you silly goose. Let's hope her teeth come in straighter than mine. We don't need dentist's bills. Now move out of my way. I have to tend to the accounting or this business will fall apart."

Feri carried his daughter into the front showroom. "Come, Eva. I'll teach you about antiques. This is called a Biedermeier armchair and this mantle clock comes from a wealthy man's home in Vienna. No, I correct myself. He used to be wealthy. Now to keep up appearances he must sell his most prized possessions."

As he walked the aisles of the shop Feri considered the new shipment that had just arrived. It held some very nice pieces and he was confident they were worth the price he paid for the lot at auction. The Bartok Gallery would provide a comfortable salary this year.

Eve squirmed in his arms. How had he been so lucky after the mess he'd made of his life? A wife, a child, this business. It was more than he deserved. Sometimes, in the evenings as he closed the shop, he would move through the aisles and re-arrange items, pick up odds-and-ends, or dust a few tables just to assure himself that they were concrete--more than an illusion.

By most people's standards he should be burning in hell for the misery he'd brought to other people's lives. Thank God he'd met Panna! Without her, he'd never have had the courage to break away from Sipos.

A cry of protest rose from the child in his arms. To distract her, he pressed the dial on the radio behind the counter. The voice of the announcer for the popular radio program, *Vasárnapi Ujság*, filled the room.

"Hungary's Minister of National Defence has announced a new crack-down along the country's northern borders and the Danube valley. Since joining the European community Hungary has endured stinging criticism of her lack of surveillance along the border with Slovakia where large armament factories have sprung up over the last few years. Ethnic divisions, particularly in light of Serbia's secret service having established their special unit called "The Wolves" to provoke violence and unrest, provides a ready-made black market for the weapons. Unnamed sources within the Ministry critical to the move, caution that tightening surveillance along the Danube will only force criminal organizations to find alternate routes to move the goods, most likely through the more isolated areas of Hungary. Arms smuggling is

far too lucrative a trade to abandon."

Yesterday's news, Feri thought as he reached for the dial to shut the radio off. Sounds like Sipos will have to get more imaginative or a portion of his business will suffer. How many times had he heard the man brag about the profits his trucks made as they moved around Eastern Europe? The big profit wasn't from the "soft" goods, as Sipos called the human smuggling he controlled. It was the "hard" goods, the guns and other armaments, that paid the big money.

A car drew up outside the shop and a man and woman stepped onto the sidewalk. Feri's heart stilled. He'd only caught a glimpse of the woman's side profile before she turned her back and walked toward the shop next door. *Impossible. It's guilt. You've been thinking about Sipos so it brought Sonja to mind.*

Eva had fallen asleep. He'd put her down on her cot in the back office and finish unpacking the new crate of goods.

***

Stan pulled two bottles of pop from the cooler. *Now here's something I don't need a translator for. This stuff looks the same in any language.* He added a few bags of junk food to his basket and joined Sonja at the till.

He held out little hope that they would find Feri. The shop where the landlady claimed to have seen him more a small grocery store than a deli. Even if Feri bought groceries here there was little chance the owner would know where he lived. From the set of her shoulders and the look on Sonja's face she felt the same way.

"He says he doesn't know anyone named Ferenc."

41

She swallowed hard, then glanced in his basket. "What have you got there? That's all junk food. Let's get some decent sandwiches and find a place along the way for a picnic."

She moved toward the back of the shop where a staff member would make sandwiches on demand while Stan paid for the items he'd selected. As he sorted through the unfamiliar coins in his hand he felt a tug at his elbow. Sonja's look was strained, her body taut with tension.

"I asked the lady in the deli. She said the man's name in the antique store next door is Ferenc. I described Feri to her. She said that's him. Stan, I think we found my brother."

CHAPTER EIGHT

When the door chime sounded Feri reached for a cloth to wipe his hands. Customers. He took a few extra moments to brush packing material from the knees of his pants. The shop was small but there were a lot of items to hold a customer's attention. Better he present himself professionally than to look like a slob.

In the showroom, he was surprised to see the man who had parked his car on the street. Dark brown hair, medium height, slim but well-muscled build. Feri's stomach muscles tightened. This man wasn't interested in antiques. His wide stance and crossed arms were the demeanour of someone used to authority. A business inspector? One of Sipos' associates?

An image of Sipos' grinning features flashed through Feri's mind. "Look at you. You're a dead man," Sipos had sneered the last time Feri saw him. "Once you have had a taste of the white powder you can never let go. Go on! Get out of here! I don't have to deal with you – I'll let the dope do it for me."

Feri drew in his breath. He had nothing to hide. Panna kept good records and paid the bills on time. He addressed the customer in Hungarian. "May I help you?"

The woman who had reminded him of Sonja stood with her back to him, examining an armoire. She turned at the sound of his voice.

In Ukrainian she said, "Hello, Feri, my dear brother."

Sonja! She stood ramrod straight, hands clenched into fists at her sides. The room receded. The air became a vacuum. No sound, no smell, no movement reached him. His sense of hearing returned first, a faint hissing that gradually grew in intensity.

43

Sonja advanced several steps and raised her hand, palm flat. *She's going to hit me.* He steeled himself, prepared for the blow.

She drew her arm back, then hesitated. Their eyes met and Feri saw pain there mixed with fury. "Go ahead. I deserve it." The sound as her palm connected with his cheek rang in his ears. Pain bloomed like a red-hot flower.

"You miserable excuse for a human being! How could you do that to me? I am your sister. I am not a whore!"

"I'm sorry. Sonja, Sonja, I'm sorry. Forgive me," he said as he reached for her. Her body remained rigid in his arms as it shook with sobs. "I'm sorry, I'm sorry," he repeated again and again in Ukrainian as he held her close and stroked her hair.

She allowed herself to be held but the tension in her did not relax.

Stan struggled to set aside his doubts as he listened to Feri's emotional appeal. Sonja might be prepared to forgive her brother, but his years as a cop made him skeptical. Feri could be asking for absolution for his own sake, to soothe his conscience, rather than offering acknowledgement to his sister that he had wronged her.

As he mulled over his feelings Stan realized his caution had nothing to do with police training. Sonja was his wife, the woman he loved deeply, and he would protect her from any and *all* danger. That included her brother if need be. Feri's hollow eyes and rake-thin frame were evidence of the physical torment his body had been through, or, Stan corrected himself, was going through if Feri still had a drug habit. For Sonja's sake, he hoped they wouldn't regret finding him.

A woman, dressed casually in a loose-fitting blouse that did little to conceal full breasts, entered the showroom from the back. Her untamed eyebrows drew together in a frown of concern as she stopped and stared in confusion at the sight of Feri holding a sobbing woman.

A soft gasp escaped her lips when she spotted the red palm print on his cheek. "Feri, what is happening? Your face...."

Feri motioned with his hand to reassure her, then gently loosened his hold on his sister. "There's someone I want you to meet, Sonja. This is my wife, Panna."

Panna stepped forward in a graceful motion worthy of a dancer. A wide, brightly coloured skirt swirled at mid-calf with each step. Her hair was pulled back to reveal a strong face that stopped short of being conventionally pretty. Stan's initial impression was that she was content with herself and would not need flattery and attention from others. She eyed Stan briefly before turning her full attention to Sonja.

Panna's dark, heavily lashed eyes brightened with pleasure when Feri introduced his sister. "How wonderful to meet you," she said in broken Ukrainian as she grasped Sonja's trembling hands in hers. "Your brother has had many bad moments about the past. You will have as well, of course. There is much to talk about between the two of you."

And I'm more than eager to hear an explanation for a couple of things myself, Stan thought as he responded to Sonja's beckoning hand to join the group. For starters, he wanted to know whose antique store they were in. And just how had Feri made a break from his past? People like Sipos didn't usually allow anyone to leave their organizations.

45

The awkwardness of the meeting was broken by the wail of a child from the back room. "Aha!" Feri's laugh had a nervous edge. "Someone is feeling left out of the excitement. Come. You must meet your niece."

CHAPTER NINE

Several hours later Stan pushed his chair back from the table and took a seat on a sofa in the small living room of Feri's apartment. Panna and Sonja lingered over their coffee at the table, nibbling spice cookies and getting acquainted over stories of Feri's childhood and baby Eva. Although there was obvious unease between Sonja and her brother, the two women seemed to have taken to each other. A burst of Panna's infectious laugh filled the apartment. It would be the exceptional person who could resist her bubbly personality.

Sonja held her sleeping niece as she made soft lulling sounds and fingered the child's delicate hands. "She has my mother's skin-tone, I think. And her slim fingers. My mother longed to play the piano." A shadow of sadness passed over her face.

The sound of cupboard doors being shut in the kitchen signalled Feri had finished his self-imposed kitchen duty. A tactic, Stan suspected, to avoid a private conversation with his brother-in-law. Like it or not Stan was going to make sure they *did* have a talk. Hopefully, he wouldn't come across sounding too much like a cop. But then again – why not?

It took several more minutes before Feri settled into a ratty armchair in the dimly lit room, a guarded look on his face. Stan realized it wouldn't be easy to get him to open up. He may as well go in fast and hard. Under the circumstances, he didn't feel any compunction about sparing the man's feelings.

"We need a frank discussion, Feri. Put our cards on the table so to speak. Otherwise, there's going to be tension that could ruin the relationship between our

47

families."

Feri nodded; a curt, defensive gesture. Shadows pooled in the hollows beneath his eyes, along the sharp edge of his nose. He glanced toward the other room then leaned closer to Stan. "I understand why you feel this way. Some things, however,... it's not easy to talk about."

"I'm a cop, remember? There's nothing you can tell me that I haven't heard before. And, I *will* assume the worst if we don't discuss it." At the blunt words Feri's head shot back, nostrils flared.

"Easy enough for *you* to say. But for me," he stabbed his index finger at his chest, "I live with the shame of what I did in my past every day. I try to forget it."

Stan nodded as he fought to control his own rising temper. "And part of that shame concerns your sister. I realize that. But I'm her husband now, Feri. I need to hear it from you how she ended up in Winnipeg, how you got out of Sipos' clutches and--"

Feri leaned forward in the chair. "That's between --"

"No." Stan raised his hand, palm out, to stem the flow of the man's words. "Hear me out. Then you can have your say. If I'm not satisfied with your explanation I'm going to be suspicious of your every move. I know *I* don't want that, and I'm sure you don't either. It's best to get it out so we can all move forward--not just you." He softened his tone. "I hope you understand where I'm coming from."

A hard look that Stan took as a challenge passed between them. He held his ground and after several seconds his brother-in-law relented. Defeated, Feri scrubbed his face with his hands, then slumped back in the armchair.

"Where do you want me to begin?" he asked in a resigned tone.

Stan allowed his body to relax. If Feri had refused to talk there was little he could have done to force the issue. "Start wherever you want. I'm not going to judge you, I just want facts so I know where we stand."

It was the usual sorry tale of a man who expected more from life than the hand he had been dealt. Hungary hadn't been the land of opportunity it had seemed from the Ukraine side of the border. When Sipos stepped forward with an offer of easy money and the fast lifestyle Feri craved, he accepted without hesitation. Although Stan had already heard the story of the meeting with Rosa Sinclair that decided Sonja's fate, it took all his willpower to control his anger as Feri related his version of the events.

"Sipos warned me that if we didn't meet with Rosa and finish the deal he would cut Sonja on her face. Disfigure her." His fingers touched the faint scar that ran from just below his right ear to the ridge of his jaw, ending at a point beneath his narrow lips. "I knew from experience that he couldn't have someone defy him without a consequence. I don't remember much about the meeting, but I do remember how thankful I was that she would escape from Sipos. Whatever happened to her in Canada would not be as bad as what would happen if Sipos decided to make an example of her."

The effort of his recital took its toll. Feri sagged in his chair, his shoulders drooped. Stan said nothing, willing the man to continue.

"At first I tried to imagine her happy...earning a good income...that somehow Rosa was what she claimed. The dream I fashioned helped a little, but not enough. Soon I could no longer remember to dream my dreams for her."

A half-hour later Feri reached the point where he met Panna. "A few times a year during the tourist season some

49

of her relatives come from the north to do shows. Gypsy groups are a big draw with Budapest's tourists, and the money is good. Panna dances for them when she has time."

Stan gave himself silent credit for having recognized Panna as a dancer. He could easily imagine her slim body moving to the vibrant Roma music that had woven its way into Hungarian culture.

Feri continued his story. "She was on a break between shows and came down to the river where I... I was sitting. I had given up on life. You know...how can a man live with himself when he's done some of the things...." He spread his hands in a gesture of hopelessness then let them dangle between his knees.

Sipos kicked me out of his network – cutting off my supply of drugs. He mocked me. Said he didn't need to make an example out of me because my habit would do a better job of it than anything he could do to me. He was almost right. That's when I went to the river...

Stan didn't push him. The fact that Feri had become so disgusted with himself was a point in his favour. Plenty of men would never think twice about how low they had sunk, especially if their steady supply of narcotics was cut off.

Feri seemed no longer aware of Stan's presence as he continued. "Panna saved my life. Gave me the courage to check into a drug program and get clean. It wasn't easy. When I came out she offered me a job in the antique store. It's her uncle's, from up north in Holloko. He runs that one but we're in charge of this one."

That settled another question for Stan. Feri hadn't married Panna to get control of the business.

"The rest is easy," Feri continued. "We fell in love, married, and now we have a beautiful daughter. I should

be a happy man, yes? But...I'm... Sometimes I think...."
He ran his fingers through his hair.

Stan had heard enough. This was a man who seemed genuinely sorry for the direction his life had taken. If one day he was called to account by the authorities, Stan wouldn't be the one pressing charges. While he could not forgive Feri for forcing his sister into prostitution, he could acknowledge the pain the man's guilt caused him. Forgiveness...well, maybe that would come later. He'd wait and see how things progressed. Ultimately, it would be Sonja who decided whether there was a relationship left to pursue.

Their conversation was cut short when the women rushed into the living room. "Guess what?" Sonja asked. She ignored her brother's presence as she directed her excitement at her husband. "Panna grew up in the north. Close to where we're going. Isn't that wonderful?"

Shit! How much had she told Panna?

CHAPTER TEN

Ujhely, Northern Hungary

The burial ground was no longer used, and rarely visited by mourners, so its undisturbed walkways and seating areas made it the perfect choice for discreet meetings. Pavel Radich's upper lip curled in derision at the sight of Misha Kormos strolling between the rows of graves in Ujhely's oldest cemetery.

Leader of the Roma Warriors. Ha! Misha was nothing more than a thieving Gypsy. Couldn't get it through his head that he was no better than the rest of the stinking rabble.

Pavel suspected that in Hungary most Gypsies were happy to assimilate and became Hungarian. A certain faction, however, went out of their way to call themselves Roma. Men like Misha nourished the grievances of the past. Not that he could be mistaken for anything other than what he was. Curly hair beginning to grey at the temples, bronze complexion, it all worked together to scream Gypsy.

At home, in Kosovo, every Albanian stood for the same thing--freeing their homeland from Serbian rule.

Pavel pursed his lips and directed a jet of spittle at the base of a mausoleum. If his aim was true and the wet mass landed where the wall met the packed dirt of the lane it was a sign the meeting would go well. It was not a perfect hit. He shrugged in resignation and stepped into the pale sunlight that brightened the gravelled walkway. As always, the KLO, Kosovo Liberation Organization, needed firepower to maintain their cause and Pavel would negotiate with anyone, even men like Misha, to get the weapons. Since the arrival of the United Nations interim mission in Kosovo, weapons had been difficult to come by, but Misha's sources had always proved reliable in the past.

Pavel did his best to ignore the pain in his crippled leg as he lengthened his stride to overtake the Gypsy. "We meet again, my friend."

Misha acknowledged him with a bright smile and friendly clasp on the shoulder. To anyone watching they were friends, or cousins meeting to visit a relative's grave. They set their steps toward the oldest portion of the cemetery and settled on a bench.

"Our business has become a lot harder," Misha said as he jammed his hands into his pockets.

Pavel removed his soft cap and stuffed it into his coat. Did Misha know about the addition to the shipment? Or was he only trying to jack up the price? "Perhaps, if your men can't handle the cargo..."

Misha's handsome face darkened. "If my men can't handle the shipment, no one can. It's as I said. The job has become more difficult. Hungary has reacted to that report of the Serbian Wolves unit provoking more violence. If it is true 20 million euro has been injected into the plan, that can pay for a lot of groups to stir up trouble. Of course, Hungary has been forced to strengthen the border patrols. We were going to bring the shipment across the Danube near Bratislava, but now – well, that route is closed to us."

"A man of your resources must have an alternate route."

"But of course! We'll have to follow the Danube to the Croat border. The Croats will be willing to turn a blind eye if the payoff is large enough. But as you know, that route is longer, more complex."

Pavel shifted on the bench to ease the pressure on his hip. To cover for the movement, he draped his arm over the back of the bench and scanned the area. All was quiet, other than a squirrel rooting through a thick drift of leaves at the base of an ancient oak tree. Pavel chose his next words carefully.

"You will be compensated for the longer route as long as you guarantee delivery."

"My people are resourceful. We know the forests and trails in every part of Hungary. Your goods will arrive. But that is not the issue."

Pavel yearned to wipe the cocky look off Misha's face. The bastard was about to wring another payment from them. "Why don't you just tell me what the issue is, my friend. Perhaps, together, we can make the problem go away."

A sharp chatter of protest erupted from the squirrel in the leaves as a usurper descended a neighbouring tree to contest the territory. After a brief exchange, and a bold feint, the resident emerged victorious. *If only it were that easy for Kosovo*, Pavel thought. *For so many years now we fight and still, we struggle, we die.*

"The problem is the shipment itself," Misha stated.

Pavel's grip on the bench tightened. This was it! The cocky bastard knew something, or was suspicious. How much had he found out, and even more important, *who* had talked? Would Misha keep it to himself, or let the information slip to the men moving the crates? "Only half the shipment is what you listed - grenades, small arms - minor weaponry," Misha stated with a grin of triumph. "The other half is landmines - a sensitive issue these days. Even the Croats may raise objections. We may have to store them until we can be sure of a safe crossing. My men have families. They won't sacrifice

54

their lives to over eager border guards for someone else's dispute."

Pavel willed himself to relax. So, they had learned about the landmines, but they wouldn't be a problem. He thought of all the good men who were willing to sacrifice their lives in the continuing underground war with the Serbs. The official conflict might be over, but until his people had their own homeland the unofficial battles would continue. That took guns and money. But it did no good to think about that now. He had to concentrate on this conversation, this problem. "And you know of such a place? A safe location?" he asked.

"Nowhere is one hundred percent safe. But there is a place we've used before--close to the border. Of course-- it will cost you more."

Misha watched Pavel's face closely. The Albanian maintained a tight rein on his emotions. Even his eyes revealed little as the conversation progressed. But there were other signs to indicate the strain Pavel was under. He had difficulty hiding the pain from what must be an old leg wound, and he smelt a bit sour--like he'd been living in his clothes for a while. Perhaps the authorities had become too curious about his actions, and getting in and out of Hungary was no longer a matter of stepping onto a train.

For a man who had seen as much action as Pavel bragged about, it would be frustrating to be relegated to the back lines, shepherding shipments through countries that couldn't give a shit about where the arms went, or who died because they did, or didn't, arrive on time.

"How far is this place from the border?" Pavel demanded.

"No more than half an hour by truck." The ruins of

55

Fuzer would make an excellent holding point for the arms until arrangements could be made for a secure crossing into Serbia. The fort had been destroyed centuries ago, but the tunnel used by the residents to escape from successive waves of invaders was still intact. It was dry and easily defensible in the unlikely event their route became known. And most importantly, his men could melt into the forests if it looked like the government was serious about controlling illegal arms shipments.

Pavel shifted again on the bench and Misha heard a growl of hunger rise from the Albanian's belly. For the first time he felt a stir of sympathy for the wiry fighter. Better to get down to the hard business of the meeting before he turned soft.

"I've heard from my contact," Pavel said. "The logging trucks will leave the border around noon."

"*Mirë*," Pavel nodded. Good.

Misha thought through the plan quickly. There would be three trucks. The shipment in the last, the one with the smaller logs on top. The route near the border was heavily forested. The last truck would hang back, then take the clear-cut parallel to the border where his men would be waiting to unload the cache hidden under the small, more manageable logs, and transfer it to the ruins.

The routine had worked many times before, although not with armaments. The fact that a portion of the shipment was land mines didn't sit well with him, but–

Pavel interrupted his thoughts. "Fifty thousand American dollars--that is the amount we agreed upon."

"For the guns, yes. But now it's a longer route, and a portion of the shipment is landmines. The price has risen by an extra thirty thousand."

"You son-of-a-bitch!" The Albanian balled the blunt

56

fingers of one hand into a fist. All pretense of friendliness was gone.

Misha's muscles tightened but he kept his voice low. "Don't even think about it. My men are watching. You tried to pull a fast one, Pavel. Don't try it again. We have our eyes and ears everywhere."

"I can offer twenty thousand extra. That is all we have."

Misha struggled to control his grin of victory. Twenty thousand would do very well. He slid a little lower on the bench and crossed his arms. "Then we have a deal. In about a week's time you should have your shipment."

The old soldier rose from the bench and limped toward the gate that opened to the sidewalk. Along his route he passed a garbage can. A stream of spittle shot through the air toward the can but fell short by several inches. The gunrunner thought he was so smart. He didn't know the half of it.

Misha watched the old man walk away, then fished in his pocket for his cell phone and punched in a number. Sipos would be pleased. Two rings later, "We have a deal," Misha stated in triumph. "Seventy thousand."

"Sounds good. Where do I send the forestry permits?"

"Ujhely. The post office there has a fax."

"You've done well, Misha. Your work will be rewarded."

After closing the connection Misha took a moment to soak in the warmth of the fading sun. Life was good. He had a faithful, compliant wife and a lively mistress. With the income from his smuggling activities he had been able to purchase a legitimate business, something almost unheard of for a Roma. And that's what he was, first and foremost, a Roma. That's where his loyalties lay. Not with Hungary, not with artificial borders. If Sipos and his organization could further the cause of the Roma he would work with him, but only as long as it benefited the Roma.

Further down the road, sometime in the future, perhaps he wouldn't need Sipos at all. The thought was sweet.

CHAPTER ELEVEN

Allan Howland groaned as he eased his long legs over the edge of the bed. Just blinking caused his head to pound. How many times had he promised himself he would cut back on the drinking? Well, it wasn't his fault this time. A phone call from an irate editor could prod any man to find solace at the bottom of a bottle, or even two, until the wee hours. Did the bastard have no concept of time zones? Budapest slept while Chicago worked, for Christ's sake.

Had he really slept so late? He considered closing the curtains to block out the afternoon sun but the effort required seemed too great.

Water. He needed water. His mouth tasted like the bottom of a toilet bowl. Not that the pipes in his miserable excuse for an apartment would produce anything remotely drinkable. And if memory served him correctly it had been a while since he'd picked up a new bottle for the water cooler.

He shuffled into the windowless kitchen, shook two painkillers from a bottle on the counter, and scanned the interior of the fridge. Cartons of half-eaten take-out, a few eggs in the tray. Nothing to drink but beer.

The hell with it. Little hair of the dog would wash the capsules down and help clear his head. He'd make sure this was his last beer this week.

He popped the cap and collapsed onto the tired sofa in the living room. What the idiots in Chicago couldn't get through their thick heads was that he *reported* news-- he didn't *create* it. Something newsworthy had to happen before he could file a story.

The last really good story he'd covered was Europe's

reaction to Hungary assuming its six-month long presidency of the E.U. He'd managed to eke out three by-lines before that spoiled prince in England married his college sweetheart and the world's eyes turned West.

"To their long and happy marriage!" Yah sure! He saluted the lampstand, often his sole drinking buddy, tipped the bottle back and finished the contents.

If he had good contacts he wouldn't have to live in this rat-hole. Contacts. That's what it boiled down to. It wasn't his fault the U.S. had shipped Bernie Gray home. The guy had always been good for a few leads in exchange for a night on the town. Bernie even introduced him to Sipos Sandor. Not that the Sandor fellow could give him much, but he sure knew how to throw a good party. Never knew who you'd meet at one of his shindigs so it made good business sense to show up for all of them.

Wars made for good stories. But the Balkans were quiet, other than the occasional skirmish that nobody cared a damn about. Maybe he should follow-up on the Gypsy scam he'd reported last month. Who was at the Canadian embassy?

He found his phone and flipped through the contact list. Louise Craddock. Shit. All he'd ever gotten out of her was third-rate material he could pick up anywhere. Well, it was worth another shot. Chicago's call hadn't been friendly. If they decided to terminate his contract he'd be stuck in this country.

By the end of the phone call to the Canadian embassy Allan forgot about his hangover. Maybe he'd hit the jackpot. Louise was on sick leave, but her temporary replacement was as green as the grass in June. A few kind words and an invite to one of the most prestigious parties in town had secured a few hours of Jordan's time.

What the hell. Such a happy incident called for a

cool one to celebrate.

Allan set his steps toward the kitchen and the bottles in the refrigerator.

***

A string quartet played softly in the background. Buffet tables sagged with expensive hors-d'oeuvres. Crystal sparkled. Waiters circulated among the guests with wine or champagne, while bartenders waited behind discreetly placed wet bars.

Sipos lounged, half-hidden, against a column at one end of the oval salon and watched the usual assortment of welcome guests, hangers-on and freeloaders continue to arrive at his monthly party. For the moment most made a show of ignoring the tables of food, although he knew before midnight arrived waiters would replenish the buffet several times.

It was a mutually beneficial arrangement. The guests stuffed themselves with food and drink, and Sipos picked their brains for any tidbits that could benefit his various business enterprises.

Mia arrived with her friend, Eliska, a newcomer from Slovakia. A stunning redhead. Her strapless gown hugged shapely curves and revealed shoulders begging to be caressed. Yes, every bit as beautiful as Mia had promised. If the Slovakian was open to supplementing her income with escort work he would give Mia a generous bonus for bringing the girl to his attention.

From his vantage point Sipos watched Eliska's reaction to her surroundings. All pretence of sophistication fell away as she first stared, then rotated in a full circle at the edge of the room. The coffered ceiling, tall Palladian windows, and parquet floors never failed to

61

impress a first-time visitor. It had been a long journey from the rotting caravan of his youth to this mansion he called home. Would he do it again? Take the risks? Break ties with his family who kept to the more traditional Gypsy lifestyle despite its degrading hardships?

The answer needed little thought. Hell, yes. He'd do it again in a heartbeat. He had only to look around this evening to know it had been worth it--every step of the way. Ten years earlier few in this room would have given Sipos Sandor a second glance. He almost wished his grandmother was still alive. "Desert your family and you will be cursed!" she had warned. A stupid old woman full of ignorant Gypsy superstition. He could still remember the stink of her shabby clothes, the stringy hair. How she had maintained such a strangle-hold on the family still baffled him. Sipos pushed away from the column to wander the edge of the room.

Most people let their pasts direct them, he reflected. It was easier to travel the road they knew. To follow in the same mindset that held first their parents, and eventually them, in the narrow rut of tradition. But when you dug the rut deep enough, it became your grave. He smiled at the thought. He'd seen quite a few graves swallow the small thinker trapped in their tradition. Sipos prided himself on thinking larger.

Two people stepped through the double doors from the garden; Allan Howland and a nervous looking young woman in an unflattering evening gown. Howland was big, with a head of curly hair worn a shade too long. In a few more years his bulk would turn to fat. He was one of the more blatant freeloaders who made a point of showing up at these parties. His main purpose for being here seemed to be the booze.

The woman was new, someone Sipos hadn't seen before. A quick evaluation was all he needed to see she was third-rate material. Even a careful makeover would do nothing for her long nose and small chin. There was only one reason for Howland to escort this one around town, she had some value to him as an informant. And if Miss Mouse had something the scribbler wanted, then Sipos wanted it, too.

He set his path across the polished floor to greet them.

"Allan, welcome!" He extended his hand and instantly regretted it. Howland's grip was damp with perspiration. "May I have the pleasure of meeting your lovely companion?"

The woman giggled and extended her hand. Rather than taking it Sipos leaned forward, gripped each of her shoulders lightly, and kissed her on each cheek. He heard her startled intake of breath as he slid his hand down the small of her back in a caress. There, he'd transferred the booze-hound's sweat where it belonged, onto his woman.

"Evenin', Sipos. I'd like to introduce Jordan Hastings. Jordan's with the Canadian embassy."

Aha! That explained Howland's interest. He would impress her with a big evening on the town, compliments of Sipos Sandor, then press her for any developing news.

"The Canadian embassy?" Sipos drew his eyebrows down in a mock frown. "I'm sorry to hear that Jordan. I'm sure your talents are wasted on the Canadians. You should be working for the French. Or the Italians. At least with them, something happens now and then. But the Canadians...." He turned his hands palms up and let the words hang between them.

Jordan rushed to defend the implication. "Oh! Not at all. I mean... well... there's usually something interesting

63

going on. Our prime minister is making a nice splash in world affairs and, well there's been a lot of," she lowered her voice, "sex scandals! Budapest is a great place and it's not like I'm bored or anything."

He took her arm and led her to the colonnade that circled the outer edge of the room. His route deliberately passed one of the wet bars. Howland followed for a few steps, then slowed at the bar. His decision made, he stopped and placed an order for a drink.

Sipos' steps never slowed. "Have you been here in Budapest long, my dear?" He tilted his head towards his companion and dropped his voice. "I hope you haven't found our European society too stilted." The tone and pacing made the words a caress.

Not long after entering his teens he had learned to perfect the caressing tactic with the help of his Aunt Darda. The older woman cackled like a chicken that had just laid an egg when he got the effect right. She hauled her skirt up over her generous thighs and fanned her crotch with the hem. "Saints help us!" she yelped. "You put your father to shame, boy."

The reference to his father stole the pleasure from the moment of celebration. Several months earlier the older man had come up against the point of another man's knife in a drunken brawl. That the fight had come about as the result of the man's daughter ending up pregnant made little impact on young Sipos. He was the result of a similar union. The hot gleam in his father's heavy-lidded eyes promised pleasure to many women, and as far as Sipos knew, there were few disappointed takers.

He set the recollection aside with the satisfaction of knowing he had celebrated his seventeenth birthday by avenging his father's murder with one of his own. Justice may have been a few years in coming, but it had been all the sweeter for having been administered by his own hand. His Gypsy heritage came with a long memory and little room for the sentiment of forgive-and-forget.

At his side, Jordan basked in the attention Sipos lavished on her. "My home is always open to members of the diplomatic corps," he murmured as he ran the edge of his thumb along her arm, "so you mustn't be a stranger. Tell me, how do you keep yourself busy?"

Pleasure brought a red flush to her face that exaggerated her pointed features. Her attempt at looking coy came across as a grimace. "Oh, well, my roommate...you know. Well, she has a boyfriend so...." Jordan floundered, then made an effort to recover. "Well, I stick to my work."

No boyfriend, no social life, the perfect source of news for Allan Howland. By the time they strolled the outer border of the room Sipos had what he wanted. It wasn't news he was happy to hear.

A fuckin' celebrated RCMP officer didn't get sent to Hungary, and by huge coincidence to Szephalom, to investigate allegations of Gypsy persecutions by Hungarian authorities. Something more was going on and Sipos had a pretty good idea what it was -- news of the latest arms shipment had somehow reached unsympathetic ears.

This shipment was the largest yet. The landmines alone were worth more than a dozen previous shipments. Add to that the special package that had been added at the last minute--well, the pay-off would be huge. There wasn't much time to deal with the threat Boyko posed, but deal with it Sipos would.

Allan Howland downed his drink. It did little to cool his anger as he watched Sipos and Jordan stroll around the colonnade. He should never have left Sipos alone with her. He cursed as he headed back to the bar. The girl was an idiot. It had taken Allan all of fifteen minutes to get what should have been restricted information from her. It would take that sly bastard half the time.

Something big was in the works and Allan was ready to stake his career, or what was left of it, on digging out the story. He ordered another scotch for himself and a glass of white wine for Jordan. By the time this evening was over the girl would spill everything she knew about the Canadian cop.

CHAPTER TWELVE

Stan leaned over his wife's shoulder to examine the highlighted map of Hungary spread on the table. Sonja and Panna had been assigned the task of planning the trip to Szephalom and from the highlights and scribbles, it looked as though they had amended the route several times.

After some good-natured pleading by Panna the night before, Feri had reluctantly conceded they could use a short holiday. It would also be an opportunity to introduce baby Eva to her numerous relatives in the north. With a little coaxing, one of Panna's cousins had agreed to run the antique shop while they were away if they could put off leaving for a few days.

The plan didn't sit well with Stan. He would have preferred not to include Panna and Feri in the trip. The necessary delay to accommodate the cousin who would run the shop also rankled. Stan wanted to leave immediately. Sitting around didn't get anything accomplished.

He tried to contain his frustrations. In the last few days their honeymoon had turned into a police assignment -- no, not really a police assignment. He was now officially attached to a branch of the British government responsible for threats to Britain's monarchy. That made him, of all things, an intelligence agent. He struggled to contain a chuckle at the absurdity of the situation. What kind of intelligence agent sat around while his wife and sister-in-law planned a family holiday so he could work on his assignment? Life was indeed strange.

He glanced at Sonja. Her life had changed in the last forty-eight hours as well. She had gone from having no relatives, other than a husband, to having a brother, and what seemed an enormous extended family by way of his marriage to Panna.

The tension he'd observed in Sonja since arriving in Budapest had eased a little, but not disappeared. He sensed her guarded feelings toward her brother, and rightly so. On several occasions Stan caught her watching Feri as he interacted with Panna, assessing the way he handled his wife and the baby. At some point Sonja and Feri would need time alone to talk through their feelings in private. On second thought, maybe the road trip would provide the opportunity they needed. In the meantime, Stan resolved to keep his eye on the situation, and his wife's emotions.

"If we take the M3 motorway north-east, to Hatvan," Panna traced a line on the map with her finger, "then take route 21, we can visit Holloko. It's a beautiful town. Life is the same there today as it was hundreds of years ago and we can visit my uncle. Then we could drive northeast to Patak where we can tour a castle-fort."

Sonja murmured in agreement as Panna's finger continued to plot a course through the town of Ujhely, near the border with Slovakia, then turn straight north to Szephalom.

"Here, near Radvany," Sonja reached forward to point at a small dot on the map, "isn't there an old mansion that's used as a hotel?" She glanced up at Stan and winked. "Wouldn't it be fun to stay there, sweetheart?"

Stan nodded and smiled but remained silent. They had tossed around several ideas as to how they would handle Feri and Panna once they arrived in Radvany. Their presence raised some problems but solved others. On the one hand, visiting Panna's family gave Stan legitimate access to older residents who may have worked at the lodge, or knew someone who did. On the other hand, it would be difficult to explore the Karolyi estate with any degree of privacy.

When they had discussed their plans the previous evening Sonja had eagerly entered into the plot to introduce the subject of the lodge. "Just make sure you suggest that Panna and I plan the trip," she stated. "I'll take care of the rest."

"Sonja, I don't know what we're headed into. Investigations have a way of taking on a life of their own when you really dig into them. Right now it all seems a bit tame but I've seen situations go from boring to ugly in an instant. I'm not sure I even want you--"

"Oh - no - you - don't." The pause between each word increased the impact. "Don't try to cut me out of this adventure now. You know I can handle myself when -- how do you say it -- the 'shit hits the fan'.

She was right, of course. She had proven she could handle herself in tense situations.

But now, as the women planned the trip, Stan's unease grew. He had been through this before. Looking at this plan objectively, what he was doing was unfair to Panna and Feri. They didn't know the second purpose for this trip. Worse yet, these were people Sonja cared about. He forced aside the nagging voice of guilt.

"A hotel? I don't think so...." Panna's brow furrowed in thought, then cleared. "Oh, you might mean the Karolyi hunting lodge. My aunt and uncle live near there. He worked at that lodge before the war. It was used as a hotel by rich people, but it's in ruins now." She tapped on the map once more. "Here's where you want to go, Stan. Szephalom. My cousin, he runs a very nice hotel there. You can do your..." She struggled to find the right word in Ukrainian, then gave up. "You could ask your questions from there."

Stan drew the map closer to examine it. "A hunting lodge, eh? I'd like to see that. It looks like it's only a few miles from Szephalom. You girls can go explore your castles and I'll spend an afternoon at Radvany."

"And I'll come with you," Feri stated as he pulled out a chair and joined them at the table. "I'd like to see it myself." Sleepy complaining from the bedroom let them know that Feri hadn't been completely successful in getting Eva down for her nap. "I heard it was very luxurious in its day. But after the war there was no call for luxury under Communism."

Stan realized it would be difficult to object to his brother-in-law's company. If either Panna or Feri misread his desire to play tourist on his own it would cause bad feelings, something he wanted to avoid. Best he remains silent for now and see how circumstances played out.

"How long will your business take?" Panna asked. She leaned back in her chair and did a little wiggle of excitement. "This is going to be so much fun. When your work is finished we can holiday."

"Depends on the people I need to speak to. If they're cooperative I can probably be done in a day – two at the most. Otherwise...." He shrugged. "The Gypsies in Canada claim persecution. The Hungarian authorities say they're part of a scam to take advantage of their own people and of Canada. One refugee is even accused of murder. I read an interesting article the other day by a fellow named Howland--"

"Allan Howland?" Feri asked.

"That's the guy. Do you know him?"

Feri snorted in disgust. "Sure, and I don't think much of him. The investigation he does for his stories is not good. His words are filtered through a... fog. If you want to know about Gypsies all you have to do is ask Panna here."

The outburst seemed overly abrupt. Feri's thin face twisted in a cruel manner so at odds with the tenderness he showed his daughter and wife. Stan filed the information away for another time.

71

CHAPTER THIRTEEN

The drive to the Gellert spa through clogged traffic had tried Sipos' patience. As he entered the once elegant facility any thought of a soothing afternoon in a hot pool vanished. It seemed every damned tourist in the city had decided to visit the Gellert today. He stepped aside as a shrieking child ran by with a dripping ice cream cone. The Romans would be disgusted with this bastardized version of their bathhouse.

Newer areas of the spa complex were a mish-mash of buildings and outdoor bathing pools connected by open passages. Although the main pool with its grand rows of polished granite pillars remained true to the Roman style visually, the artificial surf generator destroyed the ancient character of the room. Sipos gave silent thanks to no one in particular that the feature, meant to pander to vulgar tourists, operated only a few hours each day.

A sulky attendant with bad teeth shoved a locker key along with a few forints of change through a slot in the plexiglass admittance booth. Loutish behaviour. Fate seemed to have lined up events to aggravate him today.

Earlier in the morning, he had called Misha to warn him the RCMP officer, Stan Boyko, might be in the area of Szephalom. Misha dropped two bombshells. The first was that Boyko had a reservation and would arrive at Misha's hotel tomorrow. Sipos could accept that the hotel had been chosen by chance since north of Ujhely there were only a handful of places to stay that weren't crawling with bedbugs, but the second bit of news chased any idea of chance from Sipos' mind. The RCMP officer was due to arrive with Feri Sepsik.

It had been a big mistake to let Feri out of the

organization so easily. That mistake could be coming back to bite him now. When Feri demanded he be allowed to leave, killing him had seemed more merciful than allowing him to live without a steady supply of coke. Who would have guessed he'd get clean, much less team up with some cop from Canada.

Sipos had no doubt as to why Boyko was nosing around the area. Members of the RCMP were part of the peacekeeping forces stationed in the Balkans for years. An investigation into gun running would be right up their alley.

In the locker room Sipos stripped, pulled on his swim trunks and took a moment to examine his physique in one of the mirrors. The image reflected back was tolerable. Stomach taut, legs solid, but he was worried about the upper body. His biceps weren't as firm as they used to be. Old men had flabby arms. It was time to get into some sort of an exercise program, maybe even hire a personal trainer. That would fix it. But where would he find the time?

Enough of this. He closed his locker door and pinned the key to his swim trunks. Time to find out what was so important to Pavel Radich that he would break their routine and ask for a meeting.

The message from the Albanian had surprised Sipos. Their business was normally conducted through Misha, and Sipos preferred it stay that way. What had brought the old fighter to Budapest? No matter. His presence had sparked an idea for getting rid of the Canadian poking around Szephalom.

Pavel had requested they meet at the Gellert's warm pool. As Sipos threaded his way between the poolside tables sunlight filtered through the stained-glass ceiling, splashing muted pools of colour across the marble floor.

The once graceful pool that had served as a meeting place for the elite of society was now marred by a number of immersed armchairs fastened to the mosaic tile floor. Between them, tables rose slightly above the water level making it possible for people to sit neck deep in the healing warmth as they chatted, dozed, read or played chess. Stripped and patterned umbrellas, too gaudy for Sipos' taste, shaded tables where people snacked or drank cappuccinos as they gossiped or read the newspaper.

The din of conversation, shrieks and splashes mixed with the blare of traffic from the nearby street made it impossible to overhear any conversation held between two people at close range. Sipos found Pavel at a table near the far end of the pool. As they settled shoulder-deep on an underwater bench Pavel groaned in pleasure when the warmth worked its way into his worn body.

So that was why he wanted to meet at the spa. He's old and he's falling apart. Sipos shuddered at the thought of getting old. He had enough money now; he'd find a way to delay the ageing process. Men with money could accomplish anything. Overthrow governments. Buy their way into society. Why not use some of his money to slow the march into oblivion?

"I want to talk about your northern contact, Misha," Pavel stated. No preamble, no finesse. The Albanian was a boar.

"If you have a problem, get it off your chest. I warn you though, I don't want to hear petty bitching. The man's been reliable in the past." Managing a stable of whores had never been a problem for Sipos. But as his organization grew he found it a challenge to contend with the personalities of drug dealers, gun runners and people smugglers. Once he came to the realization that people were motivated by the same emotions, no matter their

74

nationality, gender or occupation, dealing with them had become less complex. He treated everyone the way he treated his women--threaten to hold back the money. The method had proved quite satisfactory.

Pavel ploughed on, oblivious to Sipos caution. "The price for the shipment was settled between us," his finger traced a line between them in the water. Wavelets churned in the narrow space, disturbing the thick pelt of hair on Pavel's chest. "But now he's changed the terms. He's demanding another twenty thousand American dollars for the job. We are men of honour, you and I." He struggled to lower his voice, which had begun to rise in anger. "The price was set."

Was that it? Did Pavel want to be sure Sipos knew of the change in terms? Perhaps he suspected Misha would pocket the difference. Or had he gotten wind of the extra package?

"Our organization cannot afford the extra twenty thousand," Pavel emphasized his statement by pounding his palm with his fist. Beads of mineral water flashed in the light. "I appeal to you. The shipment must not be delayed because of this new demand. Reconsider the change in terms. Honour our agreement."

His request delivered, Pavel slumped on the bench. Water lapped over his chin and swirled around his ears.

Sipos let the silence between them grow large, unpleasant. The old man could stew for a few moments. Despite having wrapped his appeal in the flag of honour between men, his little speech amounted to begging. The Albanian would have had to swallow a fair amount of pride to make his request. He had tried to pull a fast one by including land mines in the shipment but Sipos was confident he knew nothing about the last-minute addition of the other box added to the shipment.

Was it worth twenty thousand American dollars to have the Canadian dealt with? It was more than he would have liked to pay but still, it was tempting. If a third party removed Boyko no one could trace his death back to Sipos' organization. There was another way of looking at it, too. Ten thousand could be for Boyko and another ten thousand for Feri.

Sipos refocused his attention on Pavel. "Perhaps we can come to a compromise, my friend. Your organization is not blameless in this problem." Sipos held up his hands as Pavel began to protest. "No, no, you've made your case. Now let me talk."

Streams of water flowed from Sipos' elbows as he propped them on the edge of the pool. The old freedom fighter was just like a whore--had to explain himself rather than listen to reason.

"There is something you can do for me that will wipe out the penalty you forced us to impose. Do you have a man who can drive a logging truck? He'd have to steal it first."

Pavel considered the question, then shot a wary look at Sipos. "It could be arranged. The price will remain the same and you will guarantee the shipment is not delayed if we find such a man?"

"Well, not quite. He'd also have to take it for a special ride."

CHAPTER FOURTEEN

He'd found few research places were as dismal as the archives of the British Embassy in Budapest. Allan Howland shivered as he took in his surroundings. Seldom visited by staff, so deemed low priority for upgrading, the shelves of file boxes and envelope-stuffed cabinets had been relegated to a musty corner in the embassy's basement. A row of flickering fluorescent lights bathed the lone banquet-style table and its three mismatched chairs in a sickly glow.

He massaged his aching knees. The chair was too low for his long legs and there wasn't enough room in the cramped space to stretch them out. Out of habit rather than desire he reached for the take-out coffee he'd purchased on his way to the embassy. The brew was cold and bitter. He longed for a real drink, but until he had a handle on this story he had promised himself he'd stay off the booze.

A heavy sense of failure hung enveloped him. With his talent he should have accomplished more, made a name for himself. He could hang the blame on any number of reasons but ultimately, he knew, the buck stopped with him. If he wanted to rescue his career he'd have to make some changes. Cutting back on the liquor needed to be part of that change. The biggest part. But how did a lonely man tied to the bottle shut off the seductive voice that lured him with the promise of sweet oblivion to his problems?

He took another swig of cold coffee and told the voice to piss off. He needed to concentrate on the task in front of him. He drew another box from a shelf. Mouse droppings dotted the cover of the box. Shit! Probably the only thing he'd get out of this hole of a basement was a case of Hantavirus. He scrapped the droppings from the box with the side of his shoe and eased it open. The heavy stink of old paper rose to meet his nose but no smell of rodent piss. He pulled a handful of papers from the box and began to read.

Jordan, the secretary at the Canadian consulate, had handed him the first break for a good story he'd had in a long time. It had taken a few glasses of Sipos' fine wine, and a little probing, but he had finally coaxed the reason for the RCMP officer's visit out of her. It still galled him that Sipos may have heard the story first, but what, if anything, the oily Hungarian pimp could do with the details remained a mystery to Allan. He relegated the thought to the back of his mind where it could keep the booze monkey company. Once he got this story to the presses he'd dig around to find out what else Sipos had going. For now, he'd concentrate on Jordan's news.

A few days earlier she'd been instructed to work late in order to prepare documents so an RCMP officer could represent the Canadian government on Hungarian soil. On the face of it, Stan Boyko's assignment was to investigate a story Allan had written about extensively, the Gypsy plight in Hungary. Nothing earth-shattering there.

Allan laid on the charm in an effort to get something out of Jordan that would make the evening worthwhile. His effort paid off. As she opened up, it was clear there was more to it than that. A lot more.

She confided that while delivering coffee to the ambassador and his RCMP visitor she overhead part of their conversation. The Gypsy story was only a cover. Boyko's real reason for travelling to Szephalom was connected with the Second World War, Winston

Churchill and someone named Carl McCartney. Jordan assured him she had no idea what it all meant, and given the woman's drunken state when she shared the tidbit, he believed her.

Since the tip involved Churchill, the logical place to start investigating the background had been the British Embassy archives. He had three names he could search – Churchill, McCartney and Szephalom. A quick flash of his press card had gained him access to the subterranean archive room.

An hour later he was cold, discouraged and about to abandon the search when a half sheet of paper caught his eye. It was notice of a wire transfer of funds from England dated June, 1941. Donald Maclean was listed as the sender and Carl McCartney as the receiver. The money had been forwarded through the embassy to Szephalom for a final destination on an estate at Radvany. Bingo! He'd hit the jackpot.

A low whistle escaped Allen's lips. Any newspaper hack who had started his career on a typewriter knew the name Donald Maclean. It was synonymous with spying. This had to be the connection with the Canadian cop. But why the hell was the RCMP looking into a British matter seventy years old? Still, the connection with the British government fit.

He shoved a stick of heavily spiced chewing gum in his mouth and bit down hard. It jolted his taste buds, but not for long. They clamoured from something stronger.

The money transfer evidenced he was headed in the right direction, but now what? The next step was to figure where this bit of news led. He had to learn more about McCartney. Although he wasn't a fan of the internet, it was probably his best bet. The name Maclean was usually paired with Philby and Burgess. He'd search all three in conjunction with McCartney and see what he could shake loose from the tree of intrigue.

Upstairs, on the main floor of the consulate, he asked for access to a computer terminal. It was a long shot, but it beat having to find an internet café and handing over forints. When the receptionist demurred, he brought out the worn press card. "I'm researching a British subject for a feature article." It was amazing what the little bit of plastic and a white lie could accomplish.

"I'll call my supervisor, sir." She dialled a number and spoke softly in Hungarian. God, he hated the language. It was impossible to learn. Allan waited. His throat was parched. He needed a drink.

"Sir...sir." He'd been so busy arguing with his demon that he hadn't noticed when she'd hung up the phone. "If you'll follow me you can use the terminal in the staff lounge if you like."

Kim Philby, Donald Maclean and Guy Burgess. In hindsight, few who dug into their history could understand how their spying had been missed. The information was stunning.

The group's connection to the monarchy was through a fourth spy, Anthony Blunt. Blunt was a distant relative of the Queen and had advised the monarchy on its art collection and drawings. Anything else discussed during the cosy meetings was left to speculation. There was no mention of Carl McCartney associated with Blunt. Rather than shake the information out of the tree, he'd have to dig it from the roots. This was work for lowly researchers, not seasoned reporters. Damn the tightwads in Chicago.

He took a quick stroll around the room to loosen up his knees and returned to the computer. He'd search for another half-hour then decide whether to give up.

Philby had been part of a delegation to the U.S. and later became the SIS liaison officer in Washington with the CIA and the FBI. Interesting, but no mention of McCartney or Churchill. He was getting nowhere. He read several more reference then suddenly, there it was. His fingers stilled on the keyboard. The link was Cambridge. They'd all attended Cambridge, the recruiting ground for the Cambridge spy ring.

In 1941 McCartney had travelled to Hungary to do research on a book. While in Hungary, Maclean had sent him money. McCartney must have been collecting intelligence from Europe to bring back to his handlers in England. It fit. Oh, boy did it fit!

Allan needed a drink. Hell, he deserved a drink.

Further searching on the net turned up nothing new. Whatever it was the Canadian cop was looking for, it had to be in Szephalom or Radvany. And instinct told Allan it was a big story--a huge story. This was his last chance to make something of himself and he couldn't screw it up.

He shoved another stick of gum in his mouth and left the consulate. He'd need a car to get to Szephalom, which meant he needed money. That meant a call to his home office. The thought brought a grin to his face. Wouldn't they be surprised to hear what he had in the works?

CHAPTER FIFTEEN

When the bout of queasiness hit, Sonja struggled to hide her discomfort. She'd always had a problem sitting in the back of a car but it usually wasn't this bad. Drawing in a deep breath, she willed her shoulders to relax into the seat back. Afternoon sun shone hot through the car window. She'd give anything right now for a couple of cool cloths for her neck and forehead. Maybe she could follow Eva's lead and take a nap. The child had fallen asleep in her car seat an hour earlier.

Despite her present discomfort, the trip had been both a pleasure and an eye-opener. The previous week as they travelled from Vienna to Budapest, she grew used to the sight of McDonald's restaurants and advertisements for Coke and cigarettes. What she hadn't noticed in the western area of Hungary was poverty. Now, the further north they drove and the closer to Slovakia they came, the poorer the towns and countryside grew. It was difficult to reconcile the grandeur of the churches and mansions in Budapest and the old-world charm of the cities surrounding it with the meagre conditions they now travelled through. This seemed as poor as parts of Ukraine.

She glanced at Panna. Her sister-in-law seemed to sense her feelings.

"We enter the poorer part of Hungary now, Sonja. It is where many of the Roma people live."

"Roma?"

"You would know the term Gypsy, rather than Roma." She reached with slim brown hands to re-tie the loosened lace of her sleeping daughter's shoe.

Now Sonja understood. This was where the *Tsyhany*,

as they were called in Ukraine, lived. Sonja had never seen any of the wandering people when she was growing up, but she had read stories and she had heard about them. What she had heard was not good. She searched the landscape visible through the windows for some sign of the colourful Gypsy lifestyle of the stories. Instead of bright hues and ornamented houses, run-down shacks and littered ditches lined the highway. "Why Roma rather than Gypsy? Is the word Gypsy...." The word derogatory came to mind but Panna may not understand what it meant. She finally settled on the word 'insulting'.

"Insulting? To some, yes. But we are called Gypsy because it was thought we came from Egypt. Our dark skin, perhaps? But now we know we come from India centuries ago."

Stan turned in the front seat. "India? Really? Didn't know that."

"Yes, really." She smiled at his surprise. "Even our language, Romani, is similar to what used to be spoken in India. We wandered away from India looking for a safe home, and now look at us." She indicated the view beyond the car window with a nod. "You won't see anything that looks like the Gypsies of the movie theatre. We no longer dress in fancy costumes with dangling earrings. We no longer wander across Europe like nomads in colourful horse-drawn wagons. Most of Hungary's Roma accepted the lifestyle and language of this country decades ago. But there are still a few who cannot give up the past. They reject the settled life."

Panna shrugged a shoulder in a pretty gesture that Sonja had come to associate with her sister-in-law. The woman was a study in mobility. Eyebrows, hands, feet, every part of her body had the capacity for graceful movement.

"The wandering Roma who ignores property rights of others is not a welcome neighbour in a settled society. There is always friction between the settled people and those who remain nomads in spirit."

Feri slowed the vehicle as they passed through a village. When the well-kept square ringed with small shops and restaurants drew Sonja's attention he circled so his passengers could appreciate the striking contrast of past and present. Two teenagers lounged in front of a shop displaying cell phones and advertisements for long distance calling discounts. The store was flanked by a bakery and a shoe shop where a cobbler advertised that shoes were still repaired by hand. Further down the cobblestone street, an elderly woman carrying a mesh shopping bag entered a meat market where a variety of cuts hung in its window, and the produce shop next to it showcased freshly harvested vegetables in baskets and bins on the sidewalk.

How did the people of the village feel about the intrusion of satellite TV and cell phones, Sonja wondered. Like the Roma, did they find themselves torn between the old way of life and the need to adapt to survive and become good neighbours? She remembered her own culture shock when she escaped from Ukraine to Budapest. At first, it was hard to believe the items in the stores were really for sale and not just for show. With so many choices it had been difficult to decide which item to purchase. Several times she had walked away without buying, too frustrated and overwhelmed to make a decision.

Panna broke into her thoughts. "So, Stan is really here to investigate some Roma?"

The lie, which had initially seemed so harmless, refused to flow easily off Sonja's tongue. "Not quite," she

84

faltered. This is how Stan must feel when he goes under cover she realized. "The Canadian government needs information for an immigration hearing. Some Gyp—oh, sorry," she corrected herself, "some Roma families who came to Canada as visitors have asked for refugee status. They say they suffered persecution here. The Hungarian authorities insist their claim is a lie, that the men are criminals and want to enter Canada illegally."

Panna smiled at her. "You will not offend me if you call us Gypsy. But that is how it has always been for us. The word Gypsy is immediately connected with dishonesty, filth, cheating. It is easier to say that the Gypsy did the crime than it is to find out who is really the guilty one. We are emotional people so some Roma carry anger and hatred because of this thinking."

Sonja had to concede that her own ideas about Gypsies were exactly as Panna described. Either they were portrayed as carefree wanderers who danced and played lively tunes while dressed in colourful clothes, or they skulked about the community looking for something to steal. Panna was a clear indication of how wrong that idea could be.

The humming of the car's tires on the pavement filled the silence in the vehicle as it ate up the miles. What were they travelling into, Sonja wondered? In Budapest, the prospect of solving a seventy-year-old mystery seemed romantic. No longer. Now Stan's questions might stir up painful memories of a past layered with heartache and hate. In comparison, her unresolved feelings toward Feri seemed petty. She had been ignoring him, avoiding eye contact. She would find an opportunity to talk with him, get his side of the story, and hopefully, they could reconcile properly.

She turned her attention back to the scenery beyond

the car window but what she saw was not the dazzle of brilliant red and gold autumn leaves. Instead, a vision of families being driven away from village after village filled her mind. Did Panna share the sentiments she spoke of? Her sister-in-law had been careful not to mention her own feelings as she related the plight of her people.

It was easier now to see why Roma families paid huge sums of money to reach Canada. Unfortunately, when people became that desperate for a secure future for themselves and their children, they were easy prey for those waiting to take advantage of them. Maybe Stan actually *could* write a report on what he found here when they got back to Winnipeg.

Eva chose that moment to end her nap. The toddler's disgruntled cries filled the car. It was time to stop for a break, and not only for Eva's sake. Sonja needed a walk to clear the images from her mind.

"Hang on, Eva," Feri called to his daughter, "Papa needs a potty, too." As if confused by the adults' laughter, Eva's cries wavered, then ceased as she joined in.

The roadway widened and the poverty faded into the background, hidden behind the brighter commercial signage that signalled their arrival in Patak.

CHAPTER SIXTEEN

As he stood in a short line to buy coffee at a street vendor's stall Stan did his best to curb his impatience with the leisurely pace of the day. From the occasional hard looks Sonja threw his way he knew he wasn't being totally successful. This wasn't the way he usually worked. They had already lost three days in Budapest waiting for Panna's cousin to clear her schedule so she could tend the antique store. Today, a trip that should have taken a few hours had turned into an all-day excursion. He reminded himself there was no rush. He *was* supposed to be on vacation and no one had imposed a deadline for the investigation. Still, he was impatient to begin.

When he returned to the picnic table on the grassy banks of the Bodrog he realized Sonja and Feri were nowhere in sight.

Panna nodded to the path that paralleled the river. "It is good they have gone for a walk together. It is time to clear the air. To become brother and sister again. Here, give me that before you drop it." She ignored his weak protest as she relieved him of the burden of the wobbly cardboard tray of coffee.

Stan settled on the seat beside his sister-in-law, his hands cupped around one of the paper cups, grateful for the coffee's warmth. As she supervised her daughter's snack of animal cookies Panna played tour guide-- recounting the history of the area's leading citizens, the Rokoczi family. Their castle dominated the river view, just as their influence had dominated the history of the area in the past.

"The 'Rakoczi March' was originally composed in the

prince's honour by a Roma band leader. To play the March was long forbidden in Hungary because the tune was used during the ...." She hesitated and became frustrated as she searched for the words she wanted.

Stan stepped in. "The War of Independence?"

She sighed. "Yes, those are the words. My Ukrainian is not so good, I think."

"You don't want to hear my Hungarian."

A young mother chased her child along the river path, the two of them laughing. Their voices rose in the air, hers throaty, the child's high and piping. On their right, several men kicked a soccer ball. Despite the pleasant setting, the uncomfortable silence of two people getting to know each other stretched between Stan and Panna. He was tempted to ask how Feri had managed to kick his drug habit then shelved the idea. She might see the cop behind the question, rather than the brother-in-law. Better to keep the conversation neutral for now.

"I know next to nothing about the Roma, other than what you mentioned in the car," he said. "Do you know anything about their claims of persecution?"

"There are those who say they are persecuted," Panna replied. She hesitated, as though sorting through her words, considering each one before she continued. "Some call themselves only Roma, and push their identity. And of course there are others who say Gypsies use their race as an excuse for their behaviour. The great majority are neither good nor bad. They are just simple people who want to make a decent living, like everyone else. Those who can't find jobs sometimes turn to stealing, even robbery, out of what they feel is necessity. When parents live on crime, the child follows in the same footsteps. And so it goes, on and on."

He pressed a row of indentations along the rim of the

paper coffee cup with a fingernail. "We have the same problem in Canada with our natives."

"Forgive me, Stan, I know nothing of your natives." Panna responded. "I can tell you that the Roma have a sorrowful past. Those who do not wish to forget the past say they are treated as third-class citizens. They point out that during the Second World War the puppet government gave them over to Germany, like trash, happy to be rid of them. Germany labelled them inferiors and tried their best to liquidate them with the Jews. Instead of a yellow star, our people were forced to wear a black triangle to mark our race. More than 60,000 Hungarian Roma were deported to the extermination camps. Only a few survived that dark time."

Eva claimed her attention, leaving Stan to contemplate her words. Canada had been lucky to be spared the horrors of both World Wars. Yet, in this setting it was easy for him to feel a sense of history missing to those born in North America. Warriors in armour, princes with jewelled swords and brightly coloured boots, ladies in long silk gowns and pearl hair ornaments: all were strangers to Canada's story. As were spies and smuggled documents outlining secret negotiations with foreign rulers. All thoughts seemed to lead back to his assignment.

With a final bold display, the sun kissed the horizon. Its dying rays trapped a mirror image of the castle's red tower on the metallic surface of the river. He drew in a deep breath and let go of his frustrations. Wood smoke and harvest were on the wind and the sound of flowing water met his ears. The peaceful setting, the calmness in the air--it all came together in a defining moment. He knew this would be the image of Hungary he would remember long after the trip was over.

Feri and Sonja strolled into view, their body posture casual. The talk had obviously gone well. When they arrived at the picnic table Stan slid his arm around his wife's waist. She smiled up at him and rested her head against his shoulder for a moment, content.

"We should get going," Feri said. "I want to be in Szephalom before it gets too dark. But sometime this week we will come back here. They have a wonderful thermal bath that is worth a visit."

"You'll be staying at my cousin's hotel," Panna added as they headed for the car. "We've arranged to have supper there."

"Misha runs a small, but decent place." Feri strapped his squirming daughter into her car seat. "He's a hard one to read, though. He seems to be still trying to figure out which of the two Gypsy camps he belongs in. Also, I'd like to know where he got the money to--"

"Feri, please. Just because you don't like Misha, that doesn't mean he's not a good man," Panna chided as she slid in the back seat. "A Gypsy manages to make something of himself and right away he must be mixed up with criminals."

The muscles of Feri face hardened as he turned the key in the ignition. The engine sputtered once, then caught. "Perhaps I read too much into something I saw at a family gathering. I'll be interested in your impression of him, Stan."

To Stan's relief, a half-hour later the tires crunched on the gravel of the parking lot for the Kormos hotel. He had finally arrived in Szephalom.

CHAPTER SEVENTEEN

Thankful for the rejuvenating effects of a good night's sleep, Stan made a final sweep of his chin with the razor. All things considered, the hotel met his expectations. Rustic appearance, creaky wooden floors, rock-hard beds and noisy plumbing. But it was clean and, almost as crucial, the bathroom had been modernized. He'd stayed in far worse. He wiped the last bit of shaving gel from his face and hung the towel on the rack.

Somewhere in the span between kissing his wife good morning and emerging from the shower, Sonja had disappeared. A quick scan of the room told him her camera was missing. That figured. Photography was a relatively new passion for her; the inn and surrounding area were worthy of a photographer's attention. She may have decided to take a walk and shoot a few photographs.

As he slipped into his shoes he realized that idea was logic talking. His gut told him she needed time alone to process her talk with Feri. The night before Sonja had shared some of the conversation she'd had with Feri as they'd walked along the banks of the Bodrog River in Patak. It left Stan wondering - again - how his brother-in-law had managed to get away from Sipos so easily. Perhaps the mobster had calculated his lost drug inventory and decided he was better off without the addict. But why not kill him as an example? Something didn't fit.

Stan slid his passport and wallet into his pocket and grabbed the room key. He'd wait for Sonja in the breakfast room where they had arranged to meet Panna and Feri. He locked the door to their room and descended the staircase to the main floor.

The smell of food drew him toward a hallway leading

to the back of the hotel. As he passed through the lobby he paused. Feri's comment the day before about their landlord intrigued him: *He seems to be still trying to figure out which of the two Gypsy camps he belongs in.* Stan had met Misha the previous evening when they checked in, but other than noting the man's reserve, there had been no time to gather impressions.

He didn't want to eat without Sonja, and since the lobby was empty he decided to take a few moments for a quick look around. In the meantime maybe she would show up.

His RCMP training gave him a keener eye than most, still it was hard to get a feel for a person from the decor of a public place they owned. Morning sun from an east-facing window painted bands of light across a comfortable looking leather sofa, two tastefully upholstered wing-back chairs, and the rack of brochures that completed the lobby furnishings. Everything appeared to be of excellent quality, including the swagged earth-toned draperies on the windows. Someone had spent a lot of money and taken care with the selection, but that could have been Misha's wife or even a decorator.

A clock hung to the side of the registration desk, its ticking broke the silence in the small area. The only picture was behind the counter; Misha stood with a dour, chunky woman Stan presumed was his wife, and someone who appeared to be a dignitary.

Now that his suspicions were aroused, it struck Stan that the surroundings were a bit too neutral. No photos proclaiming Hungarian nationalism graced the walls, no flag drooped on a flag stand in a corner. Nothing stated the proprietor's pride in either his country or his Roma roots. Also missing for a boutique hotel was a hint of the owner's personality. No evidence of Misha's interests or character was visible. Rather than having satisfied his curiosity, Stan joined Feri in his suspicions. Everyday people, those with nothing to hide, generally didn't conceal themselves so thoroughly.

His stomach growled, demanding food. He glanced at his watch. It was just after 9:00 a.m. Sonja wasn't back and the breakfast buffet would be cleared soon. He'd have to eat without her. In case she missed the meal altogether, he'd pick up something portable for her, like an apple and cheese.

Only one table in the dining room was occupied. Feri, and Panna with the baby on her lap, were seated over empty plates chatting with Misha.

"*Jó reggelt* - good morning, Stan. Join us," Panna called. "Where's Sonja?"

Stan drew up a chair. "I'm not sure. She seems to have disappeared. Her camera is gone as well. I suspect she's out for a walk."

Misha nodded in welcome but remained silent. The man had an intelligent face that showed no signs of humour. Wide, dark eyes--more brown than black-- regarded Stan boldly. Broad cheekbones angled down to a jaw showing the first hint of thickening. Stan had the impression that this was a man capable of strong emotions he would keep hidden from all but the most intimate of friends. For now, Misha's expression was as neutral as the lobby of his hotel.

What are you hiding, Stan asked silently.

"We were just explaining to Misha why you're here." Feri leaned forward as though to gauge Stan's reaction to his words. "Since he grew up in the area, and is Panna's cousin, we were hoping he could introduce you to some of the people you should meet."

"Well, not really a cousin," Misha protested. "Better

to say a distant cousin. Around here everyone claims to be everyone else's cousin. It's a way of ensuring a favour when one is needed. Who do you wish to talk to?"

Instinct warned Stan off. The tense set of Misha's shoulders, the guarded look in his eyes that didn't allow them to be read. Stan ignored the question and rose to collect his breakfast from what appeared to be a decent buffet. As the proprietor of the hotel Misha was, in a sense, his host. In the normal course of events he would be attentive to his guests. Even so, his interest in their affairs felt wrong. If he was digging for information Stan sure as hell wasn't about to provide it to him.

Was it only because of the suspicion planted by Feri, Stan wondered, that he found the questions intrusive?

He spoke over his shoulder as he scooped a boiled egg from a chafing dish. "I think we've got it covered don't we, Panna? You were going to introduce me to your aunt Anna in Radvany."

Misha straightened in his chair. His eyes moved from Feri to Panna and then to Stan. "Off to Radvany are you? To Aunt Anna's?"

"Of course," Panna said. "Aunt Anna knows everything happening here in the area. If anyone will help Stan to find out the truth about those poor people it will be Aunt Anna. Don't you think so, Misha?" She wiped Eva's chin with the corner of the tablecloth and stood. "Sonja and I plan to do a tour on our own. She wants to see the ruins of the hunting chateau."

Stan returned to the table with his food and a cup of steaming coffee. "Could you hold off on that tour for a while, Panna, until I can join you? There are a couple of sites in the area I want to see, including those ruins." He offered Misha a brief smile. "I've been told the lodge was a popular place just before the war. Could be interesting."

94

Misha pushed his chair back and rose from the table. "As nice as it is to chat with you, I have business to attend to. If you need anything please just ask." He left the room in a few quick strides. Panna settled Eva on her hip and followed her cousin out at a more leisurely pace.

Feri's eyes narrowed as he watched Misha leave. "That's odd. Before you came in Misha seemed quite interested in your investigation. I thought he would want to talk to you about it."

"You told him I was an RCMP officer?"

"Of course." Feri turned his hands palms up and shrugged. "How often do I get to claim such a celebrated person in the family, I ask you?"

Stan gave him a long look over the rim of his coffee cup but remained silent. Feri was up to something. He seemed to be baiting Misha, trying to get him to tip his hand--if there was one to tip – to confirm his suspicions. Maybe there was some bad history between the two that Feri hadn't mentioned. If so, Stan didn't want to get caught up in it.

"Okay," Feri admitted with the trace of a grin on his face. "So, I wanted to see his reaction."

"And? What was it?" Stan prompted. He wasn't about to let his brother-in-law off so easy.

Feri pursed his lips. "Mmmm...you could say he was...interested. Maybe a little too interested."

"And?" Stan probed again. *Come on, come on-- talk!*

"So, I mentioned a few things we might be doing here in the neighbourhood. He seemed more interested in some than in others."

"Do you think that was wise, Feri?" Stan concentrated on buttering a piece of toast. Damn it! Feri was trying to become part of the investigation. *A God-damned amateur detective in the flesh.* For Sonja's sake, he wished he could warm up to the man, but Feri seemed to be keeping Stan at arms-length.

"Only unwise, my friend, if you are not here to investigate the Gypsy claims." Feri replied.

***

Misha rounded the back corner of the hotel and slowed his steps. *Where the hell is she?* If she were snooping around the outbuildings what would she see? He did a quick mental survey of the equipment in the sheds. Nothing too incriminating to the casual observer, *if* that's what she was. A few all-terrain vehicles, binoculars, tarps, some flares. He was being over-anxious. This shipment was the largest they'd attempted to move so far and some of the men were edgy. Their nerves were getting on *his* nerves.

There was always the chance she wasn't out for a morning walk. Panna's Ukrainian *kurafi,* that son of a whore, had made a point of mentioning his sister's skills as a detective. How she'd helped that RCMP husband of hers in another investigation. Feri had a habit of putting his nose into other people's business. Always hanging around. From the sounds of it, his sister was no better.

He chose the path that circled the water pond. If her goal was photographs, as her husband stated, the path to the pond was a logical choice. Guests loved it. A bale of barley straw added to the water each spring kept it clear enough to see trout lazing in the shallows. Red-winged blackbirds, angry at his intrusion, scolded from the rushes as he strode by.

The husband--Stan. He'd been downright evasive at the breakfast table. Feri tried to pass off some cock-and-bull story about their reason for being here, but it didn't add up. What country gave a damn about the persecution of a few Roma? His people were despised everywhere, not just in Hungary. There must be some other reason an RCMP officer wanted to nose around Radvany.

Misha's anger built as he followed the beaten trail. Damn! She wasn't here. The only other place on the property where she might go was the sheds and barn. The barn was old, made of stone, and picturesque. Maybe she had chosen to go there for photos. He'd had guests ask about the barn before. Some even wondered if he kept a gypsy caravan in it. The thought brought a snort of disgust. His colouring gave him away so he couldn't hide his ethnicity, but he sure as hell wouldn't pander to the tourists by dressing up and riding around in a caravan that had been decked out like a harlot.

The tourists wanted to see Gypsies--the colour, and what they thought of as glamour of the roaming lifestyle, even as the government tried to drive them out of the country. His people were called lazy because they didn't work, yet jobs were withheld from them. Their roads were left unpaved, doctors wouldn't tend them when they were sick, and their young women could be raped at will. His people were society's outcasts. Those that had managed to assimilate with the Hungarian population fared only a little better.

Misha reasoned that if they were treated like dogs, then they had the right to bite back. He'd bitten, and he'd bite back some more. He'd take every last forint he could make, from any source, and funnel it into the organization. With a few good men like Sipos at the top, and enough money, networks were being pulled together that would reach into the highest levels of government and society.

One day the Hungarian people would wake up and

wonder what the hell had gone wrong. It would be their turn to pay.

He left the path and cut through the small wood that bordered the meadow where the barn and sheds stood. The sun had cleared the trees, bathing the grassland in enough heat to release the scent of white clover and fescue. It was a peaceful scene, worthy of an amateur photographer's attention. He knew she was here somewhere.

The grass stirred to his left as the woman rose to her knees, camera steadied by her left hand while the right depressed the shutter release. A red admiral butterfly rose on the air current and took flight.

As she stood to join him, Misha wondered what other objects she had captured on her camera. It was a digital model. Perhaps he would have a chance to find out.

CHAPTER EIGHTEEN

"Hey, you two!" Sonja entered the breakfast room, planted a kiss on Stan's cheek and waved at Feri. "I hope I didn't miss the food." She placed her camera on the table and wandered over to the sideboard.

It had been good to get away for a while this morning, out on her own. She needed time to reflect on her talk with her brother. Sharing the conversation with Stan last night had helped sort out her feelings, but only to a point. He was an only child, born in a wealthy country. He'd never experienced being a brother, or having a sister. He hadn't struggled to provide for a family that was falling apart.

After their father disappeared Feri had done his best even though he was only a teenager. The meagre salary their mother earned could never have purchased enough food for three people, or paid for her school supplies, or the electric bill. When food appeared in the cupboard and the lights stayed on neither Sonja nor her mother asked where the money came from. Even after Feri left for Hungary money had arrived. At first in moderate sums, then later less, until it finally stopped altogether.

Their talk yesterday had ranged far. Feri explained the frustrations he experienced in Ukraine, his reason for leaving her behind, and his struggles when he arrived in Hungary. Wages for Ukrainians without legal entry papers barely paid for a room to bed down for the night. He soon gave in to loneliness and despair. Desperate to send money back home he accepted the offer of a well-paying job, deliberately not questioning why someone would pay so much to deliver parcels. Of course, he knew his employers were thugs, but that's how he had survived and provided for his family in Ukraine. Only then, it had been black market goods needed for basic living, not drugs.

When their mother died Feri hadn't wanted Sonja to join him and see what he had become. Even more, he worried that she would get sucked into the life he lived. When Sipos offered to smuggle her in, the matter seemed out of his hands.

"I was so proud of you Sonja, when you stood up to him. I never dreamt he would treat you the way he did. I think he used you to make a point with me. "

He told her of Sipos' threat if she didn't agree to meet Rosa. Sonja visually traced the scar, mostly faded now, that ran from his ear to just below his lips. She could understand why Feri feared for her if she stayed in Hungary more than if she left for Canada with Rosa Sinclair.

Circumstances and drugs had destroyed the brother she knew in Ukraine. She took comfort in the fact that he had managed to pull himself out of his abyss and become a loving father and husband.

The small woods and meadow behind the hotel had been a peaceful spot to reflect on their talk. The past should remain there -- in the past. If she could conquer the doubt that crept over her like a fog, silently, unexpectedly, until it overwhelmed her, she could leave the past behind them. They were brother and sister. As a child he had been her hero. They were on equal ground now, she no longer needed a hero, but she wanted a brother, and just as importantly, Feri wanted his sister.

She added some cheese to her plate and returned to the table.

"I was beginning to worry you'd miss breakfast," Stan said. "I wish you'd told me you were going out to take pictures."

Irritation bubbled up briefly before she quashed it. He worried about her too much. She had worked hard while they were dating and since their marriage to remind him that he was a lover and husband first and a cop second. Sometimes the cop still won out. Still, the situation they were in was bound to fray his nerves. When it came right down to it, she realized her nerves were on edge as well. She hadn't been up-front with Feri or Panna as to why they were here and how was it possible to find papers that had been missing for sixty plus years?

"Sorry. I hadn't planned on being gone so long. I took some wonderful pictures though." Shortly after they were married she and her friend Anel had taken a photography course together. It had quickly become a passion. Lately she had been toying with the idea of trying to sell some of her photos from a website that carried stock photography. The old barn and the butterflies in the meadow would make a good addition to her collection. The light had been perfect.

She poured a cup of coffee then spooned yogurt on a bowl of muesli and cut fruit. It would hold her until lunch but maybe be light enough so she didn't get car sick again.

Feri stood. "I'll leave you two. Panna will need help to get the baby ready. Shall we meet in forty minutes, in the parking lot? Radvany is only a half-hour drive."

"Does Panna's aunt know we're coming?" Sonja asked. Few people, especially older ones, liked surprise visitors. Hopefully when the questions started Panna's relatives wouldn't feel their Canadian guests were prying.

Feri nodded. "They have a phone, an old-fashioned landline, one of the few in the area. Cell service is notoriously back here in the north. Her husband, Uncle János, was the game-warden, or maybe it was the forester, for the district since shortly before the Second World War so the local bureaucrats had to let them have one." He stopped and glanced at Stan. "I would think old János knows the area around the hunting lodge very well. Maybe he would be willing to give us a private tour. We'll see you in a bit, then," he called over his shoulder and headed for the door.

Sonja ate a few mouthfuls in silence as she watched Stan brood. Something was still bothering him. "It's too many people, isn't it?" she finally asked. If the tour group for the chateau included Panna and Feri, as well as Uncle János, Stan would have little chance to look around in private.

He gave her a look of question as he recalled himself from his thoughts.

"The tour of the hunting lodge," Sonja explained. "Too many people will be in the group. Isn't that what's bothering you?"

He covered one of her hands with his and leaned close to whisper, "Sonja, I want you to be careful around Misha. Something's not quite right about him. Even Feri senses it."

His statement took her by surprise. "But I just talked to him this morning and he seemed nice. I met him while I was out back in the meadow taking pictures."

Concern clouded Stan's features. "What was he doing out there?"

"I'm...I'm not sure." What was Stan so anxious about? His worry made her uneasy, so uneasy she lost her appetite. She gave up on the breakfast and pushed the bowl aside. "Maybe he was looking for me. He just appeared along a path from the direction of the pond and reminded me that breakfast would soon be over. We walked back together."

"We'd better get a move on it if we're going to get ready in time." He tugged her hand gently as he rose from the table. "Promise me you won't go off on your own again, okay?"

She was about to protest but remembered the flat look on Misha's face in the meadow. There had been no friendliness in his tone when he reminded her of breakfast. It had been more a statement of fact that an actual reminder.

It wasn't until they were in their room gathering their gear for the day that she remembered she'd left her camera on the table in the breakfast room. Darn! She was far too careless with her things. When she'd dropped her original camera on the driveway and run over it with the car, Anel had given this one to her as a gift, specifically for this trip.

She closed her bulging daypack, shouldered it, and headed for the door. "I'll meet you downstairs, sweetheart. I think I left my camera in the breakfast room."

Stan stuffed a map into his coat pocket and raised his head to speak. She cut him off. "I know, I know, Mr. Paranoid," she grinned. "Stay away from Misha."

She hurried down the stairs to the breakfast room grumbling to herself as she crossed the sound-smothering carpet of the lobby and pushed through the door. Misha stood at the table examining the controls on the back of her camera.

"It is yours?" he asked as he extended the camera to her. "It's nice one. A wide viewing window. You wouldn't want to lose it."

She fought to control the trembling in her fingers as

she reached for the instrument. With a soft *whir* the camera finished shutting down and the shutter closed. *He was looking at my pictures! What's going on here?*

"Thank you," she murmured. Irritation got the best of her. "I think I took some interesting shots, don't you agree?" She turned and left the room, conscious of the hard look that followed her.

Stan was right. Misha had tracked her down in the meadow and he had been looking at her pictures. Was he interested in her as a person - some sick fascination - or was he spying on their entire group? Had he found out about Stan's business here? But from whom, Panna? And what would it matter to him?

She would speak to Stan about it when they were alone.

***

Feri was an excellent driver and the winding dirt road to Radvany revealed new surprises at each turn. Thick forest pressed close to the verge of the road, its blue-green coniferous trees mixed with an abundance of yellow, orange and brown leafed relatives. Fall was Sonja's favourite season. Here and there rivulets from hidden springs cut across the road, and at one sharp turn a deer sprinted back into the trees. If it wasn't for the dust she would have unrolled the window to capture the sharp smell of decaying leaves.

As the road dipped into a shallow valley Radvany's church belltower came into view above the glowing canopy of forest. She was tempted to ask Feri to stop for a photo but realized it was too dangerous on the narrow road. She glanced back. A second plume of dust from another vehicle was visible a short distance behind. A photo was impossible.

A few minutes later they entered the village; a collection of decent, simple dwellings. Feri pulled the Skoda to a stop in front of a house that appeared slightly larger than the others. A plump woman pushed open the door and rushed out to meet them, her arms open wide.

CHAPTER NINETEEN

Doing an interview through an interpreter always frustrated Stan. Being once removed from what was said to the intermediary meant the multiple layers and emotions contained within the spoken words were too easily lost, or glossed over by the third party. Even full eye contact was missing. And everyone had something to hide. He'd seen grown men tremble with shame when forced to reveal their secrets to not one, but two strangers sitting across from him. In some instances what could have been an intimate one-on-one conversation between people speaking a common language became a study in evasion. It was too easy not to trust someone who was a foreigner, someone who didn't share your background, your customs, or your faith.

He felt that frustration today as he spoke with Anna Telkes.

With Sonja's help Stan began his investigation over lunch. Panna's Aunt Anna was happy to voice her opinion and provided him with a litany of complaints perpetrated against her people. They made his blood boil. If the treatment she described came from the district level, the local bureaucracy was corrupt. If it came from the state level, Hungary had a human rights problem. Either way, Stan resolved he would file a report to Ottawa when he got home. Maybe, for good measure, he'd put a bug in the ear of Human Rights Watch as well.

As helpful as Aunt Anna tried to be about the general situation, when Stan asked about the alleged murder she became evasive.

"So many years ago...." Sonja translated. "Maybe better to leave it alone." Anna Telkes pushed the sleeves of her sweater higher on her plump arms before passing a plate of small dumplings to Panna.

There was something the old woman wasn't telling him. Should he pursue it? The refugees were his cover, not his assignment.

Unexpectedly János, Anna's husband, addressed him in halting Ukrainian. "It was not those Gypsies you ask about that killed that man." He shot a glance at his wife, and then went silent.

Surprised, Stan allowed his fork to return to his plate. The abrupt statement implied no further information would be forthcoming. The man wanted to make a point and was now done with it. Suspicion crept into Stan's mind. Were Anna and János involved in some way? Perhaps it was the older man's way of telling Stan to stop questioning his wife. But why?

The statement forced Stan's decision. If he let the matter drop he could jeopardize his cover. János had information about the murder. Stan would have to dig deeper to find out what it was. He would try and get the old man on his own and press him to open up. But for now, he would leave it alone.

"How is it that you speak Ukrainian, Uncle?" Stan asked. From the corner of his eye he saw the tension ease from Anna's shoulders. She reached for baby Eva, but remained focussed on his conversation with her husband.

János jabbed the air with his knife as he replied. "You people from North America...." His mouth bunched in distain. "You dig heels in like donkey if you have to learn other language. Here, we know two, three languages -- no problem. For me, I learn Ukrainian during war."

He went on to explain that because of his marriage to a Gypsy, he was assigned to a forced labour battalion.

"Our group was mostly nationals. Anyone Germans thought not trustworthy to bear arms." His knowledge of forestry got him placed with a work-gang clearing trees to build the defence line against the advancing Russian troops.

"My unit for most part was Ukrainians. When you cut trees all day you must speak language of your comrades to stay alive doing job," János concluded.

Forestry. It wasn't much, but it might be the opening Stan needed to turn the conversation to the Karolyi estate. With a bit of luck the old man could give him a lead on someone who had actually worked in the lodge. Stan realized János was now an important link in his investigation.

"I'm interested in seeing the old hunting lodge near here. Were you in charge of the forests around there before the war?" he asked.

"Of course. My area was very large." He grunted at the memory of his importance. "As far west as Fuzer. You like to see that old fortress, too, if you like ruins."

Stan had a moment of disappointment. Was the lodge in such a bad state of repair that János thought of it as a ruin? He pressed on. "Who owns the estate now? Would they mind if we had a look around?"

"Nobody owns it. Or everybody owns it. Depends how you look at it. Everything, lodge and property, was taken over by state after war and no one claims it except looters. Nobody looks after it." His eyes got the faraway look of someone revisiting the past. "The mansion was once beautiful, but now it rots. Beams sagging. Chimneys crumbling. It would take millions of forints to make liveable. Perhaps some day rich American comes and restores the way it was before war. Americans like luxury hotels."

108

Anna, her lips set in a thin line of anger, interrupted the conversation and addressed her husband. Bright spots of colour flamed on her cheeks and a heated discussion continued for several moments. János poured her another cup of coffee and tried to soothe her before explaining.

"She is angry I called our people looters. Perhaps she is right. Employees were not paid last wages when chateau was abandoned. She says they only trying to survive."

Stan nodded in understanding. Before the war Europe had been a class-driven society, with the lower class controlled and dependant on the upper class. As war swept across the continent many servants and employees were left to fend for themselves when the rich upper class fled. Fear and confusion would have given way to anger. "So they ransacked the estate?"

"There was not much left when they got into main building. The chateau manager, Bela Makkos, he had come before them. Most things of value gone."

There was no mistaking the feeling of disgust János felt for the manager. He practically spat out his name. "Only a few things -- books, and some things from kitchen, left. Even wine cellar empty."

Books. What kind of books? And what had happened to the looted items the employees took? The leftovers János described wouldn't have been saleable in a war situation. Stan sighed as he contemplated the remains of his meal. So many years had passed. It would be a miracle if he could turn up any clue. He was tempted to ask more questions but it might cause suspicion. Plus, even *he* didn't know what he was looking for. Better to take it slowly.

Sonja came to his aid. "Would *you* show us around the old chateau, Uncle?"

"Of course. Once was busy, entertaining place. Now it sits alone. Perhaps it is happy to have visitors to scare away ghosts. Especially pretty ones like you and Panna." He grinned, displaying several gold teeth.

Anna interrupted again.

This time it was Feri who translated. "She says before you go to that place of old ghosts you must first speak with Father Molnar. He can help you in your search for the truth about the families trying to stay in Canada."

The statement brought him back to his cover story for being there. The Chateau would have to wait. He'd need to see Father Molnar.

110

CHAPTER TWENTY

A telephone call to the rectory revealed a possible setback. A shortage of priests meant that Father Molnar led the congregations of two villages. This week he was in Vitany, near the border, and wouldn't be back in Radvany until Sunday.

"No problem," Feri said. "Use my car, Stan. I'm sure Uncle János wouldn't mind being your guide. The rest of us can get caught up on our visiting until you get back."

Stan smiled his thanks to his brother-in-law and received a grin in return. Feri was quick. He must have realized Stan needed some private time with the forester. A thought crawled through Stan's mind--had Sonja shared more than she should have with her brother, or Panna? That would explain several of Feri's comments over the past few days.

János rose from the table. "Okay, come. I will take you to priest. Now is best time to go."

The visit to the priest needn't be wasted time, Stan mused. If fortune was smiling on him, the priest would be old and have lived in the area all his life. Who knew the ins and outs of a community better than a cleric?

Get a grip, he told himself. What were the chances the visiting professor and a local priest had come into contact? He was grasping at straws.

In the car János secured the seatbelt and laced his fingers across his ample paunch. "You stay at Misha's hotel?"

The harshness in his voice caught Stan's attention. Maybe he wasn't eager to act as tour guide after all.

"It seems a nice enough place. Clean. Has a decent

111

breakfast."

János averted his face. "You are lucky man today," he murmured.

Stan shot him a look of question as he eased the Skoda onto the dusty street. Two young boys sped by on bicycles, their legs pumping like pistons. The older of the two jabbed an obscene gesture with his finger as they passed the car. Some sign language was universal. "Pardon?" Stan asked as he collected his thoughts.

"Priest, Father Molnar--you are lucky. Priest was trained in Ireland."

Stan fought to make a connection but came up empty. He turned his hand, palm up, in question. "Sorry?"

Exasperated, János explained. "He speaks English! Like you. Some questions I cannot ask for you. My Anna is proud woman. She will have my head if I say too much. But you - you must ask him about murder. Maybe he knows. Now, I say no more."

They rode in silence for a few minutes as János stared out the window. He turned to Stan. "I would wish you a contented wife with many children to keep her occupied. But I think not. Your Sonja," he grunted in appreciation, "she has spirit in her - like Panna."

***

Stan took an instant liking to Father Adorjan Molnar. Give the guy a red suit and full beard and he could stand in for North America's version of Santa Claus. Right down to the narrow glasses perched on his nose. Stan thought he'd feel comfortable spilling his guts to the priest in confession. But he was too young. He won't know anything about the guests at the hunting lodge. Stan bit back his disappointment.

The priest's grip was firm as he returned Stan's greeting in a heavy Irish accent. "You're most welcome here. It warms my heart to speak your lovely language again. Brings back memories of my seminary days on the Emerald Isle."

He led them to the rectory's cramped sitting room where he plumped the cushions on a sagging plum-coloured settee. The faded thread detailing and worn pattern attested to the passage of many years and the backsides of many parishioners. It was a dreary room. Narrow windows let in little light and the air smelt stale, heavy with the scent of old books and sheet music. Had it ever been a place of joy, or only a witness to shameful secrets whispered in the hope of forgiveness?

Images of attending church with his mother came to mind. She had been a devout woman who harboured dreams of her only child becoming a priest. Even so, his announcement that he would like to attend the RCMP academy in Regina had been accepted with pride.

The cleric gestured to a chair. "Sit, sit. A cup of tea, perhaps? On second thought, forget the tea. I can offer a not-so-fine brandy. You would do me a favour by accepting. There's been a bit of a problem today and it would be nice to unwind."

The word came out as unvind. For all his English training, the priest's Hungarian roots still came through. "Put that way," Stan laughed, "I'll accept."

Turning to János, Adorjan spoke in Hungarian. The older man shook his head, spoke briefly, then touched the peak of his soft cap with his hand and left the room. "Mr. Telkes says he looks forward to a walk. He'll be back in an hour to take you for a tour of Fuzer. He's a good man. Well respected throughout the district."

Stan suspected another motive for János absenting

113

himself. If Aunt Anna questioned him about the details of Stan's conversation with Father Molnar, he could always plead ignorance. "I understand you oversee two parishes. That must make for a large district."

Molnar grubbed around in a low cabinet, extracted the bottle of brandy and splashed an inch of the amber fluid into two glasses. "Some days it feels too large, but I doubt you came to discuss my workload." He handed a glass to Stan. "How can I help you?"

Stan briefly explained the refugee situation. "The Canadian government would like independent information on the Roma's circumstances here in Hungary. The fact that you speak English is a God-send for me."

The priest's face split into a broad smile. "And I would like to believe that my presence here is a God-send to the community. But perhaps, for both your government and my people, my presence is a mixed blessing." His round face lost its humour as he contemplated his next words.

"I think the easiest way to answer your question is to share some family histories, then you can draw your own conclusions."

Stan raised his glass in acknowledgement.

"So - let's start with a story from János' life. His father was the game warden for Count Karolyi. He was a respected man in Radvany and for a time head of the village council. According to Anna, when János announced to his father that he wished to marry a Gypsy girl, they didn't call themselves Roma back then, the father was heart-broken. And with good reason. One night, not long after János and Anna were married, she was returning home from a visit to a friend. She was grabbed from behind and beaten almost to death. As her

114

attackers beat her, they told her it was to teach her a lesson. This is what happens to Gypsies who step out of their own social circle. Anna was never able to have children after that beating."

Pain darkened the priest's face as he continued. "Her family has a sad history as well. Anna's brother died in the concentration camps during the war. Hungary's fascists jumped at the opportunity the war presented to clear out what they considered a problem - their Gypsy population."

"Would Anna's brother have been Misha's father?" Stan asked. "We're staying at Misha's hotel, in Szephalom. Panna mentioned they were cousins."

Adorjan rose and prowled the room. "No, Misha's father was a cousin to Anna, but he died in the camps as well. His death made Misha an angry, bitter man." He sighed. "When we can't give up the past... When we drag it around with us like an overstuffed suitcase.... Well, it left Misha with a deep hatred for Hungarian authority."

Aunt Anna's wariness about the murder, Janos' comments, Misha's reaction to Stan's visit to Radvany... the connection began to fall into place. "Enough hatred to commit murder? The murder that one of the refugees is accused of?"

The priest half-turned from the mantle to eye Stan. "There is... suspicion. But suspicion is not proof. Though God knows Misha would feel he had cause. Were you aware that the murder was possibly to avenge his sister's death?"

A chill crept along Stan's spine. Misha knew Stan was investigating the murder. Worse yet, he knew where Stan would be today. "If there's something – anything - you know that might help those people in Canada, our government would appreciate knowing about it. Is there

115

any chance the Hungarian authorities are so anxious to discredit the refugees that they'll pin an unsolved murder on them?"

"A chance? Not only possible but very likely." Adorjan removed his glasses and pinched the bridge of his nose. "The murder has been unsolved for many years. Pinning it on the Romas would be a way of clearing it from the books. Makkos had no relatives so --"

"Makkos? Bela Makkos, the man who ran the Karolyi estate?" The hairs on the back of Stan's neck stirred.

"The same. Didn't you know who had been murdered? Aren't you here because of Makkos' murder?"

"Father," Stan said, "could we start from the beginning?"

CHAPTER TWENTY-ONE

Allan Howland pulled the rented Mercedes to a stop in the Kormos Hotel parking lot. It would be a relief to get out of the car and stretch his aching knees. Arthritis ran in the family. Just his luck.

The car door closed with a satisfying thump. It felt good to be behind the wheel of a decent vehicle for a change. If his instincts were still sharp and he was on to a good story, maybe.... Hell, what was he saying? Of course his instincts were still sharp. It was the booze. He'd just stay off the booze. Once he wrapped this story up he'd get back to the States and dry out. Maybe join A.A. Gravel crunched beneath his shoes as he traversed the parking lot.

At the reception desk Allan ran a hand though his tangled hair then tapped the hand bell on the counter. The hotel was no Ritz but the travel bureau in Ujhely had warned him it was the only decent place before the border.

A woman shuffled from the office behind the desk. "May I help you, sir?"

What the hell? A Gypsy. A worn-out old Gypsy. How the hell did a Gypsy manage to pull enough together to own a hotel? Oh, hold on. Just because she was behind the desk didn't mean she owned the place.

"Looking for a room for the night. That, and a bit of information about the area. History. Places to visit."

"We're full for few nights. Closest hotel is Bodrog in Ujhely."

Damn. What a waste of time. He'd grab a drink, and - He cut the thought short. Not getting a room was a minor inconvenience that meant a drive back to Ujhely. It was wasted time only if he failed to get any information. Giving in to a drink? Well that would spell disaster.

"That's too bad." He propped his elbows on the counter to take some weight off his knees. "Was hoping to do a bit of touring in the district. Have a couple days and thought I'd check out a place in the area. Radvany, I think it's called."

In the hotel office Misha's finger hovered over the speed dial for Sipos' cell number. His boss put little stock in the old maxim "don't kill the messenger." When news coming in was bad, Sipos' reaction was calculated to be just slightly below his anger for not being kept informed at all. The man hadn't gotten to the top by being stupid - he knew just how far he could push an underling.

Misha weighed his options and decided to place the call. As bad as Sipos' temper would be when he heard about the Canadian nosing around, he would know best how to deal with the cop. Misha punched the button.

From the lobby the word Radvany broke through the sound of the ring. Someone - an American from his accent - was also interested in Radvany. The usually quiet district was suddenly overpopulated with outsiders sniffing around. Misha disconnected his call just as the second ring began. The distraction was a minor reprieve. Sipos could wait.

In the lobby, his wife struggled to reply to the man's leading comments. "Radvany is close but small place. Nothing to see."

"Oh, I don't want to see the village itself. My grandparents used to talk about how they spent a few weeks in a hunting lodge near there in the late 30s. Know the place?"

Rohadj meg! Misha cursed silently. This was no coincidence. First the cop, now the American. Someone

118

in his group had talked! Whoever it was would get a bullet between the eyes. The shipment would have to be delayed, maybe even called off.

Misha shot from his chair and struggled against the urge to plough his fist into the nearest wall. No matter what the outcome, Sipos would make sure someone paid. Misha had to make sure it wouldn't be him.

The office was small, too small to pace off his anger. Bracing his arms on the desktop he forced himself to draw in several deep breaths. It brought some small measure of calm to the roaring in his ears. He rolled his shoulders to ease the tension in his neck. A few more breaths and he could think clearly again.

Both the Canadian and the man in the lobby were interested in the lodge at Radvany, not the ruins of Fuzer. Did they have the location wrong? Maybe given the wrong information. Or, Misha conceded, his tension had him jumping to conclusions. They might not be interested in the weapons. But what else would bring two foreigners to an insignificant village like Radvany?

No, wait a minute. It wasn't the village they were interested in. It was the hunting lodge *near* the village. Both had mentioned how popular the lodge was just before the war. Someone had stayed there, or something had happened during that time that made it important. What had happened? Rich guests arrived, got treated like royalty and left. Nothing important there. Maybe it was one of the guests. Who had stayed at the lodge? His fingers beat a nervous tattoo on the desktop. *Think, Misha! Think!*

He quickly sifted through the possibilities. Minor aristocrats. Wealthy Europeans displaced by the advancing German troops as they overran country after country. Bored Englishmen who wanted to flirt with danger and rub shoulders with imaginary espionage agents. His fingers stilled.

That could be it. The stinking cowards at the head of the government had kept Hungary neutral during the early years of the war. The entire country had crawled with agents sent by governments to get a feel for what was happening in Europe. Now, governments everywhere were opening their archives on war-years material. He remembered reading that Russia had recently released a lot of papers. Something was here, or had been here in Radvany during the war, and someone or some government wanted it.

If his thinking was on the mark, Misha realized, more than these two would come hunting. And if they sniffed around long enough, or hard enough, he was sure they would stumble on his smuggling deals.

In the lobby, the visitor was running out of patience. Misha needed to get a look at him before he left. It might even come in handy to know if the American knew about the Canadian cop. Could be they were part of a team. He eased the door to the office open and stepped into the lobby just in time to relieve his lump of a wife, Kalara, who had only the most basic English skills so had limited vocabulary to converse with guests.

The man lounging against the lobby counter was big. His coat had seen better days and the frizzy mop of hair crowning his head needed a trim. Typical American slob. They were crude, and they were loud, but when an American got hold of an idea they were like a terrier with a rat.

Misha cleared his throat. "It's too bad we have no vacancies. I believe you were asking my wife about sites around Radvany? Perhaps I can help you."

The man winced slightly as he turned to face Misha.

Bad back, perhaps. It figured. He had a big frame but he also carried surplus weight.

The American put an extra lift in his smile as he answered. "My grandparents used to tell us kids about a rather grand hunting lodge they visited in the area. Made it sound pretty impressive. I was hoping to have a look since I'm up this way."

"Of course, of course," Misha clapped his hands together softly. "You mean the Count Karolyi estate. Our other guests, the Canadian couple, were asking about it just this morning."

The big man struggled, but failed, to hide his reaction. To Misha's surprise, it was a look of satisfaction.

CHAPTER TWENTY-TWO

Stan's grip on his drink tightened as he waited for the priest to speak. If Misha was a killer, he would view Stan as a threat. If desperate enough, he would take steps to eliminate the threat.

"The beginning." Father Adorjan slumped into his chair. "Who knows what constitutes the beginning. Does it start with man's dark nature, or in this particular case, does it start because a woman is born beautiful?" He sipped his drink and set the glass to rest on his paunch as he studied the tips of his shoes. "For me, it always comes back to the struggle between good and evil."

"Come now, Father," Stan admonished gently. "You know as well as anyone that it comes down to the choices we make. I haven't come across many criminals who were born that way." Feri came to mind. He hadn't been born a criminal, or a drug addict. Bad choices had been his downfall. A silent sigh escaped Stan as he recalled his conversation with Sonja the previous evening. Some of Feri's choices hadn't really been choices at all. In certain situations instinct takes over. The instinct to survive, the instinct to do whatever you can to help your family. Some might call it fate, or karma, or rotten luck. Whatever it was called, Stan conceded, some people were dealt a rough hand.

"You misunderstood me, my friend. I did not mean man as an individual. I meant man collectively. I was speaking of the dark nature of the ideology that sent -" Adorjan glanced at Stan. "But I digress. It's a bad habit I have. And to be able to speak with you in English, well... that's an added treat."

Despite his concern, Stan smiled. The direction the conversation had taken could prove interesting, and it fit in well with his recent thoughts on the nature of forgiveness. Still, time was a factor. A vision of Sonja being stalked by Misha as she took photographs this morning entered his mind. Given the little he'd learned from Adorjan, he had no doubt Misha had left the breakfast room with the intention of finding her.

"As I said," the priest continued, "there are many who suspect Misha murdered Bela Makkos, but it is suspicion only."

Murder. Stan's anxious feelings about Misha intensified. "When would that have happened? After the war?"

"Yes. About a year after the war."

"When Makkos was murdered, do you know if the police ever questioned Misha?"

"I doubt it. From what I hear, it isn't advisable to get on the wrong side of him. He has a number of people who are very loyal to him. And if the rumours about what lead to the murder are true, his actions would be justifiable in their eyes. You see, it's whispered that Bela raped Misha's sister. She was a beautiful young girl. It was a brutal rape and she committed suicide the next day."

Stan rose from his seat and moved to the window. Sunlight streaming through the glass warmed the chill on his skin. Rape. It was easy to see why the murder of a man who brutally raped a young girl would seem justifiable to the locals. "Did the police even investigate the death of a Gypsy girl?"

The priest ignored the question. "Before the war Hungarian society was structured by class, similar to English society. The Lords owned not just the land but the people who lived on their land. Even the servants who

123

worked in their homes. It wasn't uncommon for women working on the estate to offer themselves to the Lords to either better their lot, or to earn a little extra for, perhaps, their dowry." Adorjan grimaced as he downed the last of the brandy in his glass.

"So, you're saying that Bela may have felt he could do whatever he wished with the girl? But that couldn't possibly include rape." A movement outside the window caught his attention. János, back from his walk, and Stan had learned nothing about the guests at the hunting lodge. The old man shuffled to a bench set against the side of an outbuilding in the weedy yard. After evicting a cat that had been enjoying its afternoon nap, the old man took the animal's place and tipped his face to catch the sun's rays. Warming his aged bones. Stan still had time, but he'd have to probe more quickly.

Restless now, he moved to a tall bookcase and ran his finger along the spine of books on one of the shelves. Several English books were intermingled among the Hungarian titles.

From his seat the priest continued his story. "Aunt Anna describes Misha's sister as a beautiful young girl. Jet-black hair, slim body and a pleasing personality. Makkos, on the other hand, was a cruel man. After the war the estate was nationalized and Makkos was without a job. He became a member of the Communist Party and presented himself as the poor servant who had been exploited by the Count."

As he listened, Stan's eye continued to roam the volumes on the shelf. For the most part, the volumes in English were English classics: Lewis Carroll's *Alice's Adventures in Wonderland*, Charlotte Bronte's *Jane Eyre*. Books found in libraries where English-speaking people lived around the world. He turned his attention back to the priest.

Adorjan made a dismissive gesture with his hands as he continued. Distaste for the system was apparent on his full features. "After interrogation by the Party he was once again appointed manager of the estate, but now there was nobody to control him. As so often happens, the servant who becomes master is harsher and more demanding than the aristocrat. Shortly after the girl's death, Makkos disappeared. And that my friend," Molnar stated, "is the end of the story."

"A very sad story," Stan said. One of the book titles caught his attention: *Best Short Games of Chess*. McCartney had been an avid chess player. Stan's interest stirred; he tugged the volume from the shelf. "Do you play chess, Father?" he asked.

Adorjan glanced at the book in Stan's hand. "No, I'm afraid I don't. Many of those books were given to the rectory years ago. Personally, I think they were looted from the estate before it was abandoned. Do you play?"

"Not since my days at the RCMP academy."

A soft knock on the rectory door interrupted their conversation. János was back to collect him. Father Molnar struggled out of the embrace of the over-stuffed chair to answer the knock while Stan idly flipped the cover of the book open. A bookplate pasted to the top right-hand corner of the title page had been filled out in a well-developed, slanted hand. The signature stated the owner to be Carl McCartney. Stan almost dropped the slim volume.

As the priest greeted János, Stan riffled the pages searching for anything that would give him a clue of the owner, or his thoughts. The scent of ageing paper rose from the pages. The book seemed to want to open naturally near the centre. A broken spine perhaps? He checked, but the spine was stitched and in good repair given the age of the book.

Maybe something tucked between the cover and the spine? It would be too much to hope for. Stan thrust his finger into the narrow crevice but found nothing.

He cradled the volume in his hands and allowed it to fall open. Again it opened near the centre. Why? He gave the pages a quick scan and this time noticed the page numbers were wrong. The left-hand page was number 60 but the right-hand page was number 63. Stepping back to the window he allowed natural light to fall on the pages. A faint smudge on the corner of page 60 ... a ragged line near the spine. A page had been torn out--page 61.

János approached, his cap clutched in his hands. "Finished now? Ready to go?"

Stan nodded as he snapped the book shut. Damn! He needed time to examine it more closely.

Adorjan appeared behind János, hitching his trousers higher on his non-existent waistline. "If you're interested in chess, please take the book. It does no good sitting on the shelf. Perhaps it can teach you something." He laughed at his words as he led them to the door. "Off for a tour of Fuzer's ruins now, Janos?"

The older man nodded politely and stepped back as Stan extended his hand to the priest. "Thank you for both the book and your stories. If I think of anything else, may I call you again?"

"Anytime my good man, anytime. It is always a pleasure to meet new people and... to practise my English."

126

CHAPTER TWENTY-THREE

Stan strode quickly across the parking area to the car, causing the older man to struggle to keep up. "Do you mind if we don't visit Fuzer today Uncle? I'm sure Panna, Sonja and Feri would like to see the ruins with us."

He jammed the key in the ignition and gave it a twist. The engine caught, then died. He tried again. "Come on, come on!" The engine sputtered several times then began to purr. Thank God.

He nosed the vehicle out of the rectory's rutted driveway and turned it toward Radvany, then pressed down hard on the gas. It had been a mistake not to bring Sonja with him. For the rest of the trip he would keep her at his side no matter where he went.

"We're almost there – to Fuzer," János protested. "It is only a few miles and there is something you would find interesting at that fort. Believe me."

"Later this afternoon, perhaps. But first we'll pick up Sonja and her brother."

János pressed on. "The fort, it was under siege many times over centuries. From west by Austrians, from east by Turks. And on either side there were Hungarians who fought with equal conviction, some thinking best future lay with Turks, some thinking best chance was with Austrians."

Stan divided his attention between the history of Fuzer and the narrow road. As he entered a tight turn a loaded logging truck bore down on them from the opposite direction. The driver leaned on the horn but didn't slow his vehicle, forcing Stan several inches off the road. Bits of bark and debris from the mangled logs

127

sprayed the car as the truck disappeared in a thick cloud of dust. Stan slowed the Skoda to a crawl to regain his composure. An empty truck swept by from behind with inches to spare rocking the small car with its bow wave.

"*Hülye*. Idiots!" János spat from the passenger seat. "Logging drivers think they own road."

"They do have the advantage of their size, Uncle. You were saying about Fuzer?" He eased the car back on the hard pack and hit the accelerator. At this rate, they'd be lucky to get back to Radvany in once piece.

"Ah, yes. Fuzer. It has big secret underneath. Not just one escape tunnel, but two. One to east and other to west. Eastern route, that one is well-known," Janos' tone changed slightly, "but western tunnel...that is big secret known only to few."

Another empty logging truck loomed in the rear-view mirror. Again Stan steered the small car to the extreme right on the road. The truck driver blew his horn as he drew even with the car, then sped away.

"They are paid by load and they are anxious to make one more before sundown," János explained. He glanced back. "Here is another."

Stan had learned his lesson. As the truck, carrying a load of shortcut timber, moved to the centre of the road to pass, he braked sharply to allow the driver more room. The truck edged in front of the car, its load partially obscured by a curtain of dust. That was odd. The truck had a load, yet was coming at them from behind. The other trucks that had overtaken them were empty.

Suddenly, the wire rope holding the load parted from the chain cinch, hurling the logs directly in front of the Skoda.

Adrenalin exploded in Stan's brain as his RCMP training took over. He jerked the steering wheel to the right, propelling the car into the brush that bordered the narrow road. Several logs cartwheeled end over end across the road to smack the front bumper before ploughing furrows in the soft earth of the ditch.

"*Dögölj meg!*" János swore when the car came to a halt. A plume of dust marked the truck's passage as it crested a small hill and disappeared from view.

Stan drew a deep breath and willed his hands to release their hold on the steering wheel. If he hadn't braked when the truck pulled along side.... Around him a world that had, for a moment, been over-bright returned to focus; dust swirled then settled, sound returned. He needed air.

He grasped his door handle and shoved. A small branch jammed against the side window briefly resisted pressure, then broke. The door opened and the scent of crushed vegetation hit his nostrils.

János joined Stan at the front of the car where together they examined the damage. No major dents, but a few large scratches that could possibly be buffed out by a body shop. They had been extremely lucky.

"Strange," János broke the silence. "That truck came from wrong direction. And load was short crosscuts, not long timber. Long timber will not scatter if load releases. So now we ask--was this warning only, or attempt on your life?"

The same question had occurred to Stan. The driver would have noticed the loss of his load. If it had been an accident he would have stopped.

An object in the grass caught his attention. It was Carl McCartney's chess book. The accident must have dislodged it from the map pocket. Concerned that he had almost lost it, Stan plucked the book from the grass then parked a hip against the car's fender. The engine ticked and popped beneath him as it cooled. Overhead, a crow circled as it scolded the world for the violence it had witnessed, then disappeared into the leafy canopy. "Accidents happen, Uncle. What makes you think someone tried to kill me?"

"Misha is brutal man with much to lose. He has many friends, some at the highest levels. You come here to ask about things Misha does not want known. To stir up trouble with him is to put finger in hornets nest. Now it is done," he gestured at the dust cloud dissipating in the distance, "Hornets are out. "

Stan riffled the book's pages while he took stock of his situation. The cover story, which had been designed to allow him the freedom to investigate a war secret long forgotten, had instead ensnared him in Misha's deadly secret that was still very much alive. The door to that secret had been inched opened and Stan could see no way to close it or retreat from what lay hidden behind.

Rooks, pawns, opening gambits flashed beneath his fingers. Chess had intrigued him at the academy. Not only did it force the players to think from their opponent's point of view, it also replicated the tactical threats, traps and oversights of a crime and resulting investigation. One tactic he had learned early - always take the initiative and force your opponent into defensive moves. If that gambit didn't work, turn to slower, more elaborate strategies that accumulate steady gains.

Misha had forced this competition and made his opening gambit, but he had made a tactical error and exposed himself. It was up to Stan to reply. Two rules he remembered from his chess days stood out: keep your queen safe, and bring out your knights early.

The first was easy to follow. He would keep Sonja with him until Misha was placed in checkmate. The second was harder to apply. He had his two knights, but should he put them in play? Feri had his suspicions about Misha and seemed eager to expose him. Stan was confident his brother-in-law would be happy to help if needed. János, on the other hand was an older man, slow and unable to defend himself if things got rough.

János became restive. "Let's go! We hit son-of-bitch where it hurts. I have been trying to show you, he has secret in Fuzer. We waste time standing here." The broken branch of a beech sapling snapped under his feet as he marched around the car to the passenger side.

Stan realized he had little choice but to involve the forester. János must know something that would bring Misha to justice, and he was familiar with the area. What was more, János was his only source of information for the Karolyi estate. Like it or not, János was now a knight.

CHAPTER TWENTY-FOUR

Allan made a quick mental assessment of the hotel owner - a thug with a thin veneer of sophistication. Well-dressed, a charming smile, smooth movements; the man could pass for your favourite uncle until you looked him in the eyes. Their black depths shone with a calculating interest that went beyond casual.

Allan extended his hand. "Name's Allan Howland. I'm with a small American newspaper. Over here on a working holiday." He returned to the story of his non-existent grandparents. "Thought I'd check out that old lodge my grandparents talked about. I'd like to nose around, maybe find a human-interest story for the reader's back home."

The proprietor's return grip was firm but perfunctory, a matter of politeness only. "Misha Kormos. As I mentioned to our other guests, the estate is in poor condition. In fact, I believe it would be dangerous to enter any of the buildings. Some of the local boys play basketball on what used to be the tennis courts, but other than that there is not much happening there."

"But worth a look, for the sake of my grandparents' memories. Could you give me directions?"

A guarded expression crossed Misha's face.

He was suspicious, Allan realized, and clearly didn't want him anywhere near the estate. What the hell was going on? What had he learned from the Canadian cop?

"As I said, it would be dangerous to wander in the area alone. There are old wells, buildings falling down. If you give me a day I can perhaps find someone to guide you."

A day. Time lost. Allan didn't look forward to

driving back to Ujhely to spend a night cooling his heels. It was an unattractive place, a village really when compared to Budapest. When he'd driven through earlier he hadn't seen one decent sidewalk café. How hard could it be for this dickhead to find someone who knew the old hunting lodge? "I'm rather strapped for time, if ya' catch my drift. I'd be willing to pay someone who could take me now...." The guy was no slouch, he'd catch the meaning.

Misha smiled. "Of course, I understand. Perhaps there is something in particular you are looking for? I would be better able to direct you, or find someone to show you around, if you could be a bit more specific."

Yup, the man had caught his drift, maybe a bit better than Allan hoped. He obviously knew more than he was letting on. "I would appreciate speaking with someone who worked at the hotel during the time my grandparents were there. Someone..." he sorted through his words, cautious not to give away too much information, "someone familiar with the lodge and the people who stayed there around the time the war broke out. The old folks became quite friendly with one of the guests, a long-term renter as I understand. Know of anyone still around who worked there? Someone who might know what happened to the guy? I'd like to follow-up with him or his descendants. As I said, it would make a great human-interest story. All I need is a guide for a few hours."

Misha crossed his arms and appeared to ponder the thought for a moment. He shot a glance at the woman behind the counter; she slipped away toward the back office. A look of mild distaste settled around his mouth as he followed her shuffling figure until it retreated behind the door. "Do you know this guest's name?" he asked. "Perhaps I could inquire for you. I do know a few

133

people who used to work at the lodge. They may be able to help."

"He was a professor. Name of Carl McCartney. An Englishman as I understand it. Came here to study the Magyar history, that sort of thing. Even wrote a book about it. I would appreciate speaking to anyone who might have known him."

There was little enthusiasm in Misha's reply. "I will see what I can do. There were many eccentric people who were paying guests of the count. Perhaps there is someone who will remember this man. In the meantime, I recommend you stay in Ujhely. The Hotel Bodrog has an excellent restaurant. "

Allan sighed. It was the best he could do. He'd have to sit in a flea-bag hotel and wait for this sleazy Gypsy to contact him.

Misha extracted a piece of paper and pen from behind the desk. "If you will be so kind as to write down your name, I will contact you when I have found someone who can help." Another stiff smile.

Allan scrawled his name on the paper and made his way back to the car. What he needed now was a drug store that sold potent pain meds. His knees were killing him.

***

Misha's mouth stretched in a smirk as he watched the journalist ease himself into the fancy car. Americans. Flash their money and expect people to jump to their aid. A night at the Bodrog with its thin mattresses and stinking drains would serve him right. The guy thought he had the scent of a story and would stick with it, but there didn't seem to be any connection to the arms shipment due to arrive at Fuzer tomorrow. That was a relief.

They had probably made a mistake about the Canadian as well. Overreacted. It made sense that whatever the reporter was searching for the Canadian was after as well. Both of them arriving in the area at the same time was no coincidence. He allowed himself to smile as he punched the speed dial for Sipos. No service. Again! He grabbed the land line and made the call. It would be a better call than the one he had been about to make a few minutes earlier. All they had to do was leave well enough alone and in a few days the Canadian would grow tired of his search, or find whatever it was he was looking for. Either way, they would wait him out and then the crew could move the shipment.

To his surprise, Misha felt a twinge of regret. The Canadian would have made an interesting adversary and that wife of his--she was a good-looking woman--even though she was Feri's sister.

The smile died the moment he heard Sipos' voice on the line. His employer was in a rage.

"Incompetents everywhere! I'm *surrounded* by incompetents. I traded off good money to take out that Canadian and what do I have to show for it? Nothing. Not a God-damned thing--other than a new headache."

Misha's stomach fluttered. Sipos had already acted against Boyko. He'd made a move where none was needed! A knot of tension began to form between his shoulder blades.

Sipos continued his rant. "Get down to that forestry management company and deal with the dispatcher. Find out *what* went wrong; who screwed up. Then kill him."

Big talk, but Misha knew it would never happen. The threats, the bravado. When Sipos got angry his mind exploded. He could be reasoned with only after the vitriol was spent. One day he would push too far and Misha would strike back. That would be a day of reckoning. Who in the organization would side with Misha and who would favour Sipos? But that was one day in the future, not yet.

"I know nothing of this. Tell me what has happened," Misha demanded. Let the big shot feel the lash of someone else's tongue.

As Sipos ran through the botched plan to end Boyko's snooping, Misha's thoughts roamed on a parallel course. The cop was sure to recognize the attempt on his life for what it was, and would immediately suspect anyone he'd been in contact with in the area. He'd been asking questions of Aunt Anna and János. Although they were relatives, Misha knew they had no love for him. The old couple felt Misha had led many of his people astray. If Boyko pressed them because of the failed attack they might spill their guts about Makkos.

That *kurafi* Feri, that son-of-a-whore, was another problem. It had been a mistake to dismiss him so lightly because he worked for Sipos in the past. Ever since Feri witnessed money changing hands after a shipment he always seemed to be watching, biding his time, as if waiting for something. Perhaps he wanted to be invited into the operation, or perhaps his marriage to sweet little Panna had truly reformed him. There was also the possibility that he was waiting for proof he could take to the authorities. Hah! What authorities in this district would dare listen to anything said against Misha Kormos and his group of friends? Any attempt to interfere and they would be dead men.

On the other end of the phone Sipos ran out of venom. "I want you to deal with the dispatcher personally. We had to kill a driver to get that truck. I

136

can't trust him to get rid of the dead driver, or the truck. You take care of it."

"It was for *nothing*, Sipos," Misha stated. He had difficulty containing the anger in his voice. "He knows nothing. Boyko isn't here because of the guns."

A faint hum filled the airwaves. Then, "What are you saying? Tell me you don't believe that shit about Gypsy refugees!"

CHAPTER TWENTY-FIVE

Sonja snapped several more photos of Aunt Anna with baby Eva. The old woman, her deeply lined skin and unruly white hair held securely by an embroidered band, made an interesting contrast to the chubby-cheeked baby sporting miniature pigtails.

The family should get caught up on news without a stranger around. Sonja reasoned she could slip out for half-hour and come back without anyone knowing she had even left. The village would be a smorgasbord of photo opportunities.

Outside pale sun spread a thin layer of warmth on the failing afternoon. Along the house a beaten path lured her to the back yard. The sounds, and smells, were unmistakable--a henhouse must be close by, and undoubtedly a vegetable garden. Scenes from her childhood in Ukraine came to mind. Scrawny chickens and whatever else her mother could raise or grow in the yard had often made the difference between eating or going to bed hungry.

Chickens, a few ducks, a white goose, and something even more tantalizing greeted Sonja as she rounded the far corner of the house; large circular patterns painted on the door of an ageing shed. Faded reds, light yellow, and grey stippled with black dominated the weathered designs. She turned her camera on, then picked her way across the yard, wary of the nervous goose that hissed as it tracked her progress with sharp blue eyes.

If she could get a dozen or so really good shots she could bypass the stock photo sites and set up her own website when she got back to Winnipeg.

Quite suddenly she sensed her mother's presence. It

seemed as though the careworn woman had stepped out from behind the raspberry canes, a bowl of the sweet, red fruit in her hands, and called a greeting. Sonja tried to dismiss the feeling, the image in her mind. It was silliness. Old-country superstition.

You've done well child. It was the wind, plus the memories the garden evoked. Imagined or not, the words brought pleasure.

A car horn sounded nearby, shattering the quiet of the afternoon. As though goaded by the noise the goose launched an attack. Neck extended, wings outstretched, it flew at her. Striking again and again, it aimed for her legs as she fled back to the house clutching her camera. A frenzy of squawks exploded as chickens and ducks scattered in a flurry of feathers along her route. A scream formed in her throat and escaped as the angry bird's beak found its mark. She regained the path. Behind her the goose hissed again and beat the air with its powerful wings but it seemed to have given up the chase.

Sonja risked a glance over her shoulder without slowing her retreat. It was while her head was turned that rough hands grabbed her by the shoulders and shoved her hard against the wall of the house. Blood leapt in her veins and roared in her ears. Uncle János' face swam into her vision for a moment, his mouth set in a stern line, then Stan's back disappeared around the corner into the back yard.

"Who was it, Sonja? Are you hurt?" János demanded.

"Who?" Her tone raised a notch as fear gave way to irritation. "It was a goose, Stan! A big angry goose." She shrugged off the man's hands. "What did you think, for God's sake?" His protectiveness had crossed the line into paranoia. She'd have it out with him here and now.

Stan reappeared with a sheepish look on his face. It served him right. "Stan, you're really over-reacting here."

A tremor ran through the arm he placed around her shoulders and his grip was overly tight. The knot of anger in her chest melted. Something had happened this afternoon, something that disturbed him.

He rested his cheek in her hair. "Is Feri in the house?"

She nodded and swallowed a lump of fear. They reached the street. "The car! Dear God, what happened to the car?" Several fresh scrapes ran across the bumper and up onto the hood.

Stan ignored the question. "I want you to take Panna and Aunt Anna into the kitchen. Ask them to make coffee, entertain them with a goose story--whatever. I need to talk to Feri without alarming them. I'll explain it all to you later."

A protest formed on her lips but Stan tightened his grip on her shoulder. "Please, Sonja. Not now. I promise I'll explain everything to you later."

He opened the door to the house and gently pushed her inside. She'd have to wait until they were alone.

Stan smiled his thanks to Sonja as she ushered Aunt Anna and Panna into the kitchen on the pretext of preparing coffee and a snack for the men. She could occupy them for fifteen minutes, tops, then they would be back with the refreshments.

In the car on their trip back he'd confided as few details as necessary to Uncle János to explain his true reason for being in the area. The old man had listened carefully and asked few questions. Hopefully Feri would do the same.

As soon as the women entered the kitchen, Stan

launched into his story. He quickly recounted his meeting at the consulate, leaving out particulars of what the documents might be--including who was interested in them. He then went into a more detailed account of his meeting with the priest and the events on the ride home. Feri didn't disappoint him; his brother-in-law sat quietly, nodding slightly from time to time. When Stan finished, Feri rose from the sofa and strode to the window for a look at the damage to his car.

"Damn it! Misha must have his filthy hands involved in something really big. I'm sorry Stan. I shouldn't have mentioned you were an RCMP officer." He slammed his fist against the windowsill. "If he thinks you're here to investigate what he's up to, I know he would try to kill you. You're *sure* it wasn't an accident?"

Stan nodded. That much he knew for sure. Anything else was speculation. "If it was Misha, and I stress the "if", he must have some powerful contacts in the area. Getting his hands on a logging truck at such short notice says a lot."

"Oh, he's got the contacts all right. If it wasn't an accident then it could only be Misha. I've seen a few things in the past that didn't seem right, and Uncle János and I have had a conversation or two." He glanced at János, who grunted in agreement.

"Feri, Stan and I we discuss some things," the old man said. "I told him about smuggled goods in Fuzer tunnel."

Feri turned from the window, his hands on his hips. "Good. Whenever we're up here I keep a close eye on Misha. I'm sure the local police are also involved in what he's into. I've been trying to figure out what I can do without getting myself jailed, or killed." He paused for a moment, considering his next words. His eyes moved

141

from Stan to János, then back to Stan. "I've seen him a few times with someone... well, someone from Budapest. If I'm right, Misha is involved with Sipos Sandor."

The name hit Stan with the force of a blow. Sipos Sandor. He recalled Sipos' eyes the day they had seen him on the street in Budapest. They'd put him in mind of a hungry animal. If Misha felt threatened by Stan's presence in the area he may well contact Sipos.

A burst of laughter and clink of cups issued from the kitchen. The women would be back in a few minutes. Now was not the time to go off on a new train of thought. He needed to stay focussed on Misha.

Stan had formed the nucleus of a plan but he needed help to flesh it out. These men had knowledge of the area, and the people involved that could make or break the undertaking.

"I'm dealing with two problems here, so--first things first. Misha."

He voiced his concerns in very broad strokes. They'd have to report the accident to the police in Ujhely. If they didn't report it, the silence would alert the attacker to their suspicions. That task could wait until morning.

"Okay. Now, the second problem-- I need to find out what's on the missing page of Carl McCartney's chess book. I can phone my request to Winnipeg, but with poor cell reception here, I'll need access to either a fax or email to get a reply that actually shows me the information. What's closer, fax or email?"

Feri was quick with his reply. "The closest is Misha's hotel. He has both, but that won't work."

Stan was unable to control the expletive. "Damn!" He could imagine Misha lounging against the doorframe of his office, overseeing the messages Stan sent and received. "Anywhere else?" This wasn't the backside of

142

the moon. There must be facilities for email nearby.

János provided the needed information. "Ujhely. They have email and fax machine in post office."

"Ujhely it will have to be then." A bit of a drive, but it also worked in with the next step he felt they needed to take. "Is that where the police station is for the district?"

The old man nodded.

There was also the matter of where they would spend the night. To stay away from the hotel would alert Misha to the fact they suspected him in the so-called accident. Better that they returned to the hotel. It would throw him off guard and possibly gain them time before he tried again.

"But I have a problem with going back to the hotel. We may be putting Sonja, Panna, and the baby in danger. Got any ideas on that Feri?"

"I can suggest nothing for Sonja, but the easy solution for Panna and the baby is to have them stay with Aunt Anna so they can show the baby off to a few more relatives. It wouldn't be unusual." He snapped his fingers. "Come to think of it, they could go back to Budapest. The shop could easily have a minor problem that needs tending to. I'll arrange for train tickets while we're in Ujhely."

The solution sat well with Stan. Panna might kick up a fuss, but a white lie from Feri was warranted under the circumstances. That left Sonja. She could go back to Budapest with Panna, but Sipos was in Budapest. Chess strategy said to protect your Queen. Stan preferred to keep her close, as long as she understood the danger she could be in.

The kitchen door opened. Sonja shot him a charged look and he winked in return. He had countered Misha's move, he was in control again. But how long would it

take Misha to resume the game?

CHAPTER TWENTY-SIX

Stan checked his watch then punched in the phone number for Inspector Mark Willis, his contact at Criminal Intelligence Services in Manitoba. It would be late morning in Winnipeg so he should be in his office. Mark was more than Stan's superior officer; he became a good friend to both Stan and Sonja when Stan was injured on his first assignment under Willis' supervision. If anyone could offer advice on the situation with Misha, and fast-track finding the missing page in the chess manual, it would be Mark.

With pleasantries out of the way Stan brought his friend up to date.

"The locals here have known for years what's been happening but those who aren't earning their living from the smuggling have learned it's safer to keep their mouths shut. They're a marginalized group. The government has persecuted and harassed them for decades so they're wary of the law at the best of times. Plus, if Misha is involved with that Sandor character out of Budapest, this is high-level stuff. I don't think what passes for law enforcement in the area can handle it."

"I'll make some calls," Willis replied. "Our criminal intelligence branch will know who to contact in Europe. CSIS has been involved in the Balkans for years. Come to think of it, I seem to remember a watch notice recently that came out of the area you're in. I'll check it out. Now, how's that other matter going?"

Stan ran through the details of his visit with Father Molnar, then made his request. "I need to see what's on pages 61 and 62. I suspect there's an image, or a diagram, since a paragraph on page 60 makes reference to one. I'm not sure which page it's on – 61 or 62, so I'll need both. I can pick up your message and any image you send to my regular email account. I'll access it from Ujhely."

"With the name of the publisher we should have the information in a day--maybe two. Anything else we can help you with? Or should I even ask?"

"I think that about covers it. Not much you can do from Canada. I wish I'd played more chess at the Academy. If you can offer any tips about the image you'll be sending, please feel free to offer away."

"Will do. And Stan, I'm really sorry about this other business. I thought a side trip to an old Hungarian estate would add a little excitement to your honeymoon."

Stan laughed. "When I get back I'm going to add a paragraph to the procedural manual--never give out your holiday plans, or a contact number. But having said that, I am intrigued with what's in those papers the British are trying to find."

He cut the conversation short as Sonja joined him at the car. The setting sun had robbed the heat from the day. He gathered her in his arms, as much to share her warmth as to offer his.

"I feel bad, Stan. Panna's wondering why she can't come back with us to the hotel tonight, then bring the baby back to visit the cousins tomorrow. She thinks we've ganged up on her."

"She's safer here. I hope you didn't mention anything?" He felt her head shake in denial. They'd managed to spend a few minutes alone before supper and Stan had given her the unedited version of what had happened earlier in the afternoon, both at the rectory and on the return trip to Radvany.

"I'm sorry I doubted you about Misha," she stated.

146

"What are we going to do now?"

"We're going to go back to the hotel and talk about the terrible accident we almost had and how the truck didn't even stop. We'll make a fuss about going to Ujhely in the morning to report the driver. Then, we'll go up to our rooms and Feri will rumple his bed and come and spend the night in our room.

"Don't expect me to sleep!" Her words were muffled against his chest. She snuggled closer.

"No, my love, I don't imagine any of us will get much sleep." He stroked her hair and felt her body relax against his. The scent of her, familiar to him now but still intoxicating, rose from the soft skin of her nape. Her warmth was more than pleasant. It was a shame Feri would be spending the night in their room. "Tomorrow we'll go into Ujhely and I'll have a word with the police detachment there, I'll check my email, and we'll take a trip over to Fuzer. From there we'll have to play it by ear, as they say."

Sonja laughed. "Play it by ear," she repeated. "Stan, some of your English expressions are just plain silly."

He smiled into the dark. He'd kill to protect her. His smile died. Misha had killed because someone had harmed his sister. He would have felt just as justified for his actions.

The door to the house opened, allowing Panna's voice to escape. "Feri, sometimes you make me very angry. Why are you so stubborn tonight?" For a moment the figures of Feri, Panna and Eva were captured in the light of the room behind them.

Feri's reply was carried away on the evening breeze. Then the door closed and he joined them in the car. "That was tough. Just wait until she learns she's going back to Budapest on her own." In the half-light of the moon the

147

whites of his eyes glowed. "She will be *really* pissed."

Plans were reviewed as Stan followed the forked beam of the Skoda's headlights along the sinuous curves of the road back to Szephalom. "Have you ever been to Fuzer castle, Feri? I'd like to know what we can expect."

"I've seen it a few times, but I've never been there. It sits at the top of an old volcano dome just behind the village of Fuzer. It's a hard climb up a steep slope to the castle walls--part of the reason I haven't visited yet. The castle has an impressive history. It was attacked many times by both the Turks and the Austrians. It would be unusual for a castle like that not to have an escape tunnel, so the one to the east is no surprise. But the west tunnel that Uncle János mentioned--now that is unexpected."

Stan made a clicking sound with his tongue. "That's too bad. We'll have to take Uncle János with us, then. Let's hope we get in, see what we have to see, and get out again without meeting anyone."

Both Misha and his wife were behind the reception desk when they arrived at the hotel. The manager seemed relaxed as he greeted them; his wife nodded and shuffled through a door that undoubtedly led to the office. Her spirit, if she had ever had any, had long left her.

Stan gave full rein to his creativity while he detailed the truck incident, removing the presence of Uncle János by making Feri the passenger.

"No, the driver didn't even stop," Feri confirmed Misha's query. "And it happened so quickly I didn't have a chance to catch the company name on the truck."

"We'll have to report it to the police in Ujhely, tomorrow," Stan said. "Can you tell us where we can find the police station?"

Misha, his arms braced on the counter, shook his head solemnly. "This is a very distressing thing to have

148

happen to one of my guests. It must definitely be reported. Would you permit me to take you to the police station in the morning?"

"No need, Misha," Feri replied. "I know the town, and I have a few errands to run for Aunt Anna. Just general directions will do."

Tension seeped from Stan's shoulders when Misha nodded. He reached for a pad of paper and drew a simplistic map, then offered his sympathy again as the group headed for the stairs to their rooms.

When the door to their room shut Stan let out a loud breath. "The man has ice-water in his veins! I didn't see one iota of concern in him. It makes me wonder how he can be so confident."

"My poor Stan," Sonja murmured from where she had flopped on the bed, her head propped in the hollow of her hand. "You come from Canada, so you are an infant in these matters. Misha is unconcerned because he has the local police in his pocket. Or, perhaps we can even extend that if Feri is right, and say that *Sipos* has the local police in *his* pocket. Misha knows that nothing will come of the fact that you report the accident. Still, to keep our cover going, we must go to the police and file the report."

Her accent had crept back into her words, Stan noted. She was nervous, which may account for the fact that she had only picked at the food on her plate during supper. Still, she had been determined to return to the hotel.

Stan turned the lock on the door and advanced on his wife, miming a monster about to attack.

"*Stan!*" she shrieked before dissolving into giggles.

"Your brother will have to wait," he replied.

149

CHAPTER TWENTY-SEVEN

Morning sun though worn draperies pulled Allan Howland from a troubled sleep. He showered under a thin stream of water, shaved, and made his way to the breakfast room of the hotel. Several minutes later he pushed his plate aside. The eggs had been decent, but the pan-fried potatoes were doused with paprika, a spice he detested. Frustration and boredom added to his bad temper.

Damn this delay! What to do for the next few hours? He'd given it his best shot, but Ujhely had little to hold his interest. The baroque church was unremarkable and the statue of Louis Kossuth third rate. His hotel room was small to the point of being claustrophobic, the bathroom drain stank and all the TV channels were in Hungarian. Not realizing he would have down-time, he hadn't thought to bring along any reading material in English. The desk clerk could only offer a two-year-old copy of *Time* magazine.

If the Gypsy didn't phone by noon he'd find his own guide to take him to the hunting lodge. The story of his grandparents having stayed there prior to the war was a pretext anyway, so he didn't need someone who knew the place when it was a hotel. He could nose around as good as any snoop he knew but he'd prefer to keep his cover story intact to raise less suspicion.

Who knew what that damned cop was up to in the meantime? He could have found whatever he was looking for and be on a flight back to Canada by now. The thought stuck in Allan's craw.

Over a second cup of bitter coffee he tried to reason out what could be at the lodge. If McCartney was, in fact, a spy then it stood to reason there could be papers, code books, pictures, maps -- ah yes, Pulitzer material. But first, he had to get at it.

He paid his breakfast bill and settled into one of the two sagging chairs in the dusty lobby. From this vantage point he could watch the action, the little there was, on the street. A couple of women pushing baby strollers and a troop of kids burdened with backpacks provided limited entertainment during the first fifteen minutes. At this rate, he'd be brain-dead by the time Misha called.

A pack of dogs raced by on the other side of the street, falling over each other trying to sniff the ass-end of the lead dog. He drew a notebook from his pocket to work the idea of mongrels chasing a bitch in heat into an analogy on society. As he put his pen to paper a trio on the sidewalk, two men and a woman, caught his eye. He recognized one of the men, the scrawny one, although it took a while to place him. He was one of Sipos Sandor's people. Allan hadn't seen him lately, but a year or so ago he'd been a regular at Sipos' parties.

What was the guy's name? Had something to do with weasels, which seemed appropriate. No, not weasels, ferrets. He snapped his fingers. That was it! Feri!

Allan glanced at his watch--10:00 o'clock. Should he take the chance of missing Misha's phone call to trail the group? If Sipos had something happening in Ujhely it could be interesting, maybe too interesting to pass up. And if Misha did call while he was out, Allan reasoned he could always call him back.

As he struggled out of the chair a thought hit him. Christ! Of course Sipos had something going here. He'd gotten the same information out of Jordan, the secretary at the Canadian embassy, as Allan had. And Sipos hadn't believed that crap about why the Canadian cop was here, either. The couple with Feri could even be the Canadians. The other guy could be the cop!

Allan grabbed his coat from the back of the chair and headed out the door, his reporter instincts humming. Sipos must have sent his scrawny foot-soldier to have a snoop around.

The trio moved with purpose for several blocks before entering a nondescript three-story stone building on the main street. The emblem of the Republic above the door identified it as a government building, but it was only when he spotted several letter boxes out front that Allan realized it was the post office. He loitered outside for a few minutes, then pushed through the door.

During his travels Allan had come to the conclusion that public buildings in Europe generally fell into two categories. Either they were bright and modern or old and dreary. The Ujhely post office fell into the latter category. The feeble glow cast from high wall sconces did little to brighten the large, drab room. A bank of rental boxes shared space along one wall with a poster board plastered with tattered notices. Half a dozen wickets lined the adjacent wall but only one was manned by a bored postal clerk who appeared to be on her last legs. None of the people waiting in line were Feri or the couple.

Allan scanned the rest of the room. Both phone booths were empty and no one stood filling out forms at the short counter under the lone window. The group had disappeared.

The only other exit from the room was a small, frosted glass door near the rental boxes. A sign in Hungarian covered the lower portion of the window. The passage to the public rest rooms, perhaps. He crossed the marble floor, grabbed the handle and pulled. To his

152

surprise the door opened to reveal not a corridor to the bathrooms, but a high-ceilinged room that had been converted into a public computer space. And better yet, the trio was clustered around a computer.

Allan smiled. The machine next to them was unoccupied. Chances were he could sit right beside them and the skinny character wouldn't recognize him. Allan Howland in evening dress bore little resemblance to Allan Howland in casual clothes.

He settled into the chair in front of the screen and groped in his pocket for some coins to plug the machine's meter. This better be worth the effort it would take to actually get logged on to the internet.

***

Stan skimmed his fingers back and forth across the keyboard as he waited for the internet connection. The computer was old and the connection incredibly slow. To add to his irritation some jerk chose to use the computer immediately next to them.

He kept his voice low when he spoke. "What time did you say the train left for Budapest, Feri?"

His brother-in-law pulled an envelope from his jacket pocket to examine the contents. "Four o'clock."

Sonja sighed, the sound almost a groan. "Oh, boy. Panna's going to be so mad."

Stan shot his wife a warning glance. "Let's not get into it again. I have half a mind to send you back with her. I want to hear you promise me--" The computer connected with the internet and Stan navigated through the programs to his mailbox. There was a short note from Mark Willis in Winnipeg but no mention of the missing pages from the chess book. Mark's message was cryptic and included an international telephone number.

"Jim is aware of your situation. If you need to, give him a call, especially if any part of the shipment came through the former Eastern Bloc."

Stan programmed the number into his cell phone. Hopefully, the contact was local, and he'd be where there was cell service, but the number could easily be anywhere in Europe. He had no clue what the number combinations were for international calls.

He closed his mailbox on the computer, and then the program. Local or not, he was glad to have a contact through CSIS, the Canadian Security Intelligence Service. At least he had someone to call if things got out of hand with Misha or Sipos.

"Stan?" Sonja's hand on his arm recalled his wayward mind.

"It's just a contact number. Nothing yet on the pages from the book." He got up from the computer terminal and nudged Sonja further into the middle of the room. Feri followed. "That means we'll have to wait until later to go to the chateau." He checked his watch. "We've got roughly five hours before we need to be back here for the train. I'll re-check for messages then. Feri, does that give us enough time to get to Fuzer, then back to Aunt Anna's to pick up Panna?"

"Plenty of time. But we'll need Uncle János. He's the one who knows what's going on up there. Trouble is, if we stop at the house to pick him up, Panna will want to come with us."

Stan reined in his irritation. The entire investigation had become too complicated. Energy was being spent keeping people out of the way rather than getting the job done. Once Panna and the baby were on the train he could relax a bit, but that still left Sonja....

154

He flipped his phone open. No connection. Either the post office was a stone building or service was out. He passed the cell to Feri. "Could you take this outside and see if you can contact the house. Ask János to meet us somewhere? Say, at the church in the village? We can pick him up there."

"Right. I'm on it." Feri left the computer room to make the call.

Stan reached for his wife's hand. "Sonja, I want your promise that you'll do exactly as I say this afternoon. No questions, no arguing. Okay? These men aren't playing games. They're serious and so am I. If you don't promise, then I'll send you back to Budapest with Panna."

Sonja met his gaze with a neutral look, but a shadow passed in the depth of her eyes. Her lips parted in a smile that did little to reassure him. "Of course. I will do as you ask."

Her reply was forced, but it was a promise of sorts, and the best he could expect from this strong-willed woman. She was a brave, passionate, fiercely loyal wife who dreamed the naive dreams of most young wives. If she was too headstrong for her own good, he would have to make sure she remained safe. He was prepared to do that, no matter what.

CHAPTER TWENTY-EIGHT

"Stan! Look!"

Feri's shout yanked Stan from his thoughts. On the road ahead a small cavalcade of logging trucks crested a rise and bore down on them. He shot a glance at his brother-in-law who gripped the steering wheel so hard his knuckles shone white. In the back seat, Sonja uttered a plea for protection. *Hospody pomozhy menee.* God help me.

The loaded vehicles swept by in a noisy roar, well on their own side of the road. Stan took several deep breaths as he willed the image of tumbling logs from his mind. "Let's all try to relax. Misha won't pull the same stunt again. Besides, we told him we reported it. Once could be an accident, twice makes it too obvious someone's got it in for us."

"We're going to hold you to that thought," Sonja said. The attempt at levity dispelled some of the tension in the car.

As the vehicle sped toward Radvany Stan sorted through each possible outcome of their trip to Fuzer castle. He had to make decisions now. No use trying to figure out a strategy once the action started.

"You know," Feri said as he eased the car around a bend, "Misha has paid the local officials to turn a blind eye to the smuggling. It will be useless, maybe even dangerous to contact them if we find anything illegal in the tunnels."

"I agree. But János is sure there's something going on. If we find any evidence, I'll use the contact number I received today from Canada. I just hope the "Jim" that's mentioned in the email is local. He can take care of it."

"And if he isn't?" Sonja asked.

"If he isn't...well, at least someone, presumably with the power to do something, will be aware of what's happening in Fuzer." He could do nothing. He was a foreigner with no jurisdiction. That was one decision made.

Next decision...what to do with Uncle János. It would be best if the old forester could point out the route they should take and then stayed out of danger. Best scenario would be that he stayed at the base of the slope to the old fort. If the climb was as difficult as Feri indicated, the older man's presence could be a liability. Maybe both János *and* Sonja could stay with the vehicle.

No, that was wishful thinking. There was no way she would stay behind and Stan conceded to himself, reluctantly, that he preferred her close to him where he had some power over the situation if all hell broke loose.

The road began its descent into the shallow valley that cradled a small collection of villages near the Slovak border. Above the tree tops the belltower of Radvany's church pierced the sky. János would be there by now, waiting for them.

Sonja stirred in the backseat. "This is a beautiful part of Hungary, isn't it? Yesterday I wanted to take a picture but someone was behind us. I didn't dare ask Feri to stop."

Instinctively, Stan turned in his seat to look. A plume of dust marked the presence of another vehicle on the road.

At the edge of the village Feri turned into the first alley they came to and cut the engine. "Wait here. I'll get János." He headed back to the entrance of the alley, stopped to let a Mercedes speed by on the main road, then disappeared from view.

157

So that's the car that was behind them. A pretty expensive vehicle for this area, Stan thought, as he rolled down one of the Skoda's windows. A cool breeze entered, a welcome relief from the heat trapped in the sheltered alley.

A brood of chickens emerged from a backyard and began to peck at invisible bits of food lodged in the weeds. Somewhere nearby pigs rooted, their nasal snorts marking their progress. Fall was the season of harvest; pigs and chickens included. Soon activity in the backyards and animal pens would be limited to roaming cats and tattered plastic bags flapping in the wind.

Several minutes later an excited dog, tongue lolling, tumbled into the alley followed by János and Feri. The mutt abandoned the pleasure of human contact to give chase to the chickens as the men slid into the car.

"Hallo, my friends," János said as he settled into the seat beside Sonja. "Now we share adventure."

Stan smiled as he exchanged a glance with Feri. The old man seemed to enjoy the prospect of helping expose Misha's activities.

They approached Fuzer from the south. Stan sucked in his breath at his first glimpse of the castle. The ancient volcanic cone that held the fortification aloft towered over a thick carpeting of forest around its slopes. Red-roofed houses with tidy, fenced yards clustered at its base.

"I should have brought gun," János said. "This forest is game preserve. There are dangerous animals here. Wild boar, too. I brought hunting knife instead." He patted the knife in its sheath on his belt.

Stan heard the silent implication in János' words--*and dangerous men.* Their small group was unarmed, save for a hunting knife, while the smugglers would have weapons. If they stumbled onto any illegal activity they would be sitting ducks.

The thought had crossed Stan's mind that morning. After some thought he reasoned that the smuggling had been going on for some time with few noticing it, or at least exposing it. That meant the men kept a low profile and weren't likely to bring attention to themselves. Especially to a few late summer tourists. Moreover, he was only going to have a look, not to make an arrest.

"You have a gun, Uncle?" Sonja asked. "I'm surprised the government allows you to keep private weapons. In Ukraine it was forbidden."

"A shotgun. From back when I was forester. Communist authorities were incompetent. They classified gun as old, no longer good weapon, and let me keep it. But I could not buy manufactured cartridges. Only home made cartridges were allowed for me. To make is very tedious job. Especially pellets."

"And you still have powder and fuse at home?"

"Yes, but now if I can buy shells then I buy. It does not pay to fiddle to make those things. Sometimes I still hunt--elk, boar." He shrugged a shoulder. "To hunt with shotgun is good challenge. Wealthy men still come, like in old days, and pay big money for trophy kills. But they bring telescope rifles. Hunting is not sport anymore with that type of gun."

At the edge of the village an empty gravel lot doubled as a parking spot and picnic area. A thick border of trees in a riot of autumn colours screened the parking area from the village. Stan suspected the buffer served to shield the villagers from the constant coming and going of day-trippers as much as to beautify the place.

When Stan broached the subject, János brushed away any suggestion that he point out their route and stay with the vehicle. "No. First we must climb by footpath. Later we will see where tunnels are. Not easy to find." He gave a curt nod in the direction of the castle.

Stan conceded defeat. Sonja met his eye and winked as she grabbed her camera off the backseat then swung into step with the older man. Despite her carefree manner he realized her face held little colour. "Coming?" he called to Feri.

Feri popped the trunk of the Skoda. "I'm getting my jacket. There might be a wind up there."

The path rose steeply then levelled off at a viewing platform. The group stopped to give János a chance to catch his breath. Even in its dilapidated form the fortification was majestic. Gigantic stones in the curtain wall had been laid with an accuracy that, in Stan's view, rivalled modern building practices. "Parts of the walls are in ruins, but there's no rubble. What's happened to it?"

Feri provided the answer as he shrugged into his jacket. "Building material can be hard to come by here, and it's expensive. My guess? Over the years people just took the smashed stones and made their homes from it. Look there," he pointed to several buildings in the village below. "Those foundations are probably made from castle rubble. And some of those walls over to the right? That's stone from the fort."

After a strenuous fifteen-minute climb they entered the fortress through an imposing reconstructed stone arch. Although János hadn't complained during the trek he was breathing hard. He found a seat on a massive stone immediately inside the entry. Stan kept an eye on him as Feri and Sonja made a hasty inspection of the castle's courtyard area.

A watch tower and gothic chapel were the only structures still intact within the crumbling outer walls. The courtyard appeared empty, but to Stan's trained eye the numerous partial walls of the castle's service buildings, the excavated dungeon and cellars, even the trees and shrubs, all could provide places of concealment. He would have preferred to be among a swarm of tourists in case the smugglers had posted a look-out. As it was, if Misha was near, or had described them to his accomplices, they were vulnerable.

While János caught his breath Stan joined Sonja at the north wall. The view was spectacular. Beyond the forest at the base of the cone sunlight painted the harvested landscape in shades of gold. He reached for Sonja's hand. As she glanced at him and smiled he noted again how pale she seemed. "You okay?" he asked. Before she could answer Uncle Janos joined them.

"It is across those open spaces that invaders came in old times from Slovakia," János stated. "Today, it is smugglers who invade the castle. They come with drugs, and guns, and desperate people hidden in trucks. They think we will all turn blind eye because we are also Gypsies and there is blood tie. But now it comes more and more. Even some who help Misha do not like what they see. It is time to put stop to this business."

So that's why János had decided to help. The shipments were coming in more often. Perhaps becoming larger. Guns were a lucrative trade, particularly with a ready market in Bosnia or Kosovo. One of Misha's men must have complained to János, or asked for advice.

A sudden thought sent a chill down Stan's spine. The note from Mark had specifically mentioned the former Eastern Bloc. The break-up of the Bloc had resulted in lax supervision of nuclear material. Items were missing across Eastern Europe. Rumours were rampant that for enough money material could be smuggled out disguised as innocuous items or along with small weaponry

161

shipments. Stan remembered one CSIS report that mentioned plutonium flakes embedded in smoke detectors, and a mysterious substance called "red mercury" that commanded a whopping half-million dollars per kilogram.

Feri picked his way along the curve of the wall. "Everything looks okay here. Uncle János, where are your tunnels?"

"Come. We go to chapel first."

Deep in thought, Stan trailed behind the group. Wars were expensive, especially underground wars where black marketeers sold weapons at inflated prices. It took massive amounts of money to buy arms for an insurgency. In Africa, diamonds were smuggled to fund weapons purchases. In Europe, when so-called freedom fighters could get their hands on it, small amounts of nuclear material like cesium-137, or cobalt-60, were smuggled along with arms shipments to finance the acquisition of more weapons. There was no shortage of interest from third parties in the Middle East for the extra cargo. If word had leaked down through the smuggling chain that radioactive material was in the shipments passed through Misha's pipeline, some of his men could have turned against him.

He reached for Sonja to draw her close. If his suspicions were on the mark, this was the last place any of them should be.

***

Allan Howland turned the Mercedes around just before the Slovak border and headed back to Fuzer. How had he lost track of the group? The cop had probably realized someone was following them, but where had they disappeared?   Allan slammed his palm against the steering wheel.   His chance at a big story and he'd screwed up!

He slowed the car to a crawl at the edge of Fuzer then spotted the parking area for visitors to the castle, set back in the trees. The dusty Skoda sat in the lot. He'd found them. Damn! Other than the Skoda, the lot was empty. That meant there were no other visitors at the castle. Not that it mattered. They were probably just sight-seeing, and there was no way he could make the climb. Not with his bum knees.

He followed the line of the track up the mound to the castle and spotted four figures nearing the top. How long would they be up there nosing around--an hour? That was a lot of time to waste just sitting in a parking lot while they played tourist.

Misha, that Gypsy at the hotel, was playing him. He was too fuckin' curious. For some reason he didn't want Allan to go to the chateau. Was it to keep him out of contact with the Canadian? Did Misha know what the cop was after? Allan considered a few options then decided he'd go back to the hotel and see if he could coax more information out of the proprietor. Maybe mention that he'd run into the cop, see what the reaction was. Anything was better than trying to climb that hill.

CHAPTER TWENTY-NINE

Musty, cool air washed over Sonja when Stan pulled the heavy chapel door open. Her sweater wasn't warm enough. She should have followed Feri's example and brought her coat from the car; even on the climb up the foot-path a light breeze had raised gooseflesh on her arms. She hung her camera around her neck and hugged herself to ward off the chill, then regretted it. Her breasts were sore, so sore she had almost pulled away when Stan put his arm around her on the battlements. Too much coffee, or chocolate. She'd have to cut back.

The interior of the chapel disappointed her. Unlike other churches she had seen on their vacation this one had no vaulted ceiling or ornate tabernacle, no painted scenes or even tracery on the casements. Two lancet windows along the long wall, and one window at either end let in just enough light to pick out the heavy stone altar and the remains of stone ribs on the wall pillars. Other than a few carved canopies that may have held statues in the distant past, there was not much to hold a visitor's interest.

János moved with silent determination to one of the pillars near the altar stone and put his weight against it. To her surprise, it moved to reveal the entrance to a tunnel.

"People would flee to chapel if castle overrun by attackers. This is last place they would defend, then survivors could escape through tunnel." Light from the chapel illuminated only the first few feet of the narrow passageway. He waved them forward to the opening.

Sonja hesitated. Other than János, they had no idea what to expect farther down the tunnel. The pillar had

164

moved with surprising ease but made enough noise to alert anyone who might be waiting for them in the dark. Stan seemed to trust János, but he must be relying on a policeman's instinct. They had no real proof of where his loyalties lay.

Under the guise of letting Feri move forward she stepped to Stan's side. A tug on his hand passed the message to lean closer. She whispered: "He seems sincere, Stan, and I certainly like him, but if we go in there... Do you really trust him?" Her unease grew as she gazed into the black void of the entrance.

"I do," he whispered back.

Feri braced an arm on either side of the opening and peered in. "Uncle, how long is it? We have no idea what is happening farther down there."

Sonja gulped, and nodded her agreement.

"No, no. Is okay," Janos stated. From a pocket of his baggy trousers he removed a tiny flashlight. When he twisted the handle a beam of light stabbed the darkness of the tunnel opening. "There is nothing hidden in this one. They will be in other tunnel. The tunnel that goes in west direction." He stepped into the path of the flashlight beam.

Sonja's unease blossomed into fear. She struggled to swallow the heavy lump in her throat. Stan had done this before in his undercover work--put his trust in others--and his instincts hadn't let him down in the past. For her it was more difficult. Her thoughts ran wild as panic set in.

What if they had been lured here? Feri had lied to her when he told her he would smuggle her out of Ukraine for a better life in Hungary. And she had trusted him -- yet he betrayed her in the worst way to pay off a gambling debt. He could be working in league with János now. She thought she had forgiven her brother. But if

165

she had, how could she be second-guessing herself?

Nausea scalded her throat. It was Feri and János who had led them to this place. Feri could still work for Sipos, and Sipos was the head of the smuggling ring. János was a Gypsy and Gypsies couldn't be trusted. Feri had made sure Panna hadn't come with them to Fuzer. He knew it was a trap!

She forced herself to draw a ragged breath and swallowed hard but it wasn't enough. Mist formed in her peripheral vision and a faint buzz gathered in her ears. She was going to faint.

Stan's voice brought her to her senses. "Sonja, I want you to stay behind me. Feri, keep an eye on our rear." She nodded and forced herself to back up a few steps.

"Stan," Feri said as he drew something from his coat pocket. A gun. Sonja froze. This time she wouldn't go meekly. She wasn't the same girl he had betrayed in Budapest. Her muscles bunched as she prepared to launch herself at her brother.

Feri grinned sheepishly as he handed the weapon to Stan. "Just thought I should bring it along in case of an emergency. I have a feeling it will be put to better use in your hands." From his other pocket he withdrew a magazine of ammunition.

Strength fled from Sonja's limbs. She sagged against the altar stone. In doubting him she had let herself down. Giving in to that double would destroy any chance they had as a family. She vowed it wouldn't happen again.

Stan checked the magazine and inserted it into the grip. He slid the magazine release back into position and stuffed the gun into his waistband before looking up. "Thanks. Ready?"

Feri placed an arm around her shoulders and guided her toward the opening of the tunnel. "Now my brave sister, you have your husband in front of you and your brother behind you. What more could you ask for?"

The words were an attempt to lighten the mood on his part, but not to her. She sought out his eyes in the dim light. "Nothing. I have everything I need."

He met her gaze with a strong one of his own and gave her shoulders a small squeeze. The muscles in his throat worked in a deep swallow. Sonja turned and followed Stan into the tunnel.

János shuffled ahead of the small group, the light from his flashlight bathing the uneven floor and walls in a yellow glow. After the first few feet the tunnel angled downward several degrees. As they progressed, the air took on a thick quality, and she was aware of the damp on her skin and the changed smell. Cobwebs brushed her hair and small chattering creatures fled ahead of the beam. Suddenly the ceiling, which had been so low in places that it had forced them to hunch over, rose several feet. Was that bats she heard fluttering overhead? A shiver ran through her.

Stan stopped to run his hand over the wall. "It's almost smooth. And look at the floor." Sonja glanced down, then toed the accumulated litter. "It's smooth too. Like glass."

"I've seen this type of thing before. We went to Idaho on vacation when I was a kid and toured one of these. It's called a lava tube. When they carved out the escape tunnel centuries ago they must have hit a portion where lava flowed at one time."

His voice echoed off the stone walls, easily heard if anyone were listening ahead. She found herself straining to catch a sound that indicated they were not the only ones in the passageway.

János grunted and set out again; they followed.

167

Several hundred feet further along the floor levelled out and curved to the right. Sonja sensed freshness in the air, then faint light filtering in from an opening ahead picked out suspended dust motes. The escape tunnel had come to an end but it was only by crawling on their hands and knees that they could stand in sunlight among massive boulders on the slope of the volcanic cone. She drew in a great breath of clean air and suppressed the urge to shout for joy.

Feri's head and shoulders emerged from the narrow opening, a grin on his smudged face. "Have I ever told you how much I hate narrow places?"

She answered with a smile of her own and extended her hand to him. He gripped it and emerged to stand beside her.

"So, you see east escape tunnel." János stated with some pride.

"And the other tunnel, Uncle? The west tunnel?" Stan asked.

The forester gestured along the slope. "Now we must walk, and climb toward west. The path is not so easy."

CHAPTER THIRTY

Allan tapped the small handbell on the counter of the Kormos Hotel. It took several minutes before the woman - had Misha actually said she was his wife? - shuffled out of the office to answer the summons. He marvelled at the lack of animation on her round face. There was no indication she even recognized him from the day before. A robot, programmed to give minimal service.

"Your husband around?" he queried. He was convinced Misha knew what the cop was looking for. Why else would he stall him from going to the hunting lodge? Could McCartney have cached looted war treasures on the property? Paintings, even small ones, that went missing during the war commanded millions from collectors today.

"Misha not in hotel." She turned to leave.

Shit! Misha could be at the lodge right now. "Expect him back soon?" The words came out sharper than he would have liked. He needed a drink to calm down.

She tilted her head slightly as she scrutinized him. A spark of interest flared in her black eyes. "Maybe."

What was she doing? Giving him the evil eye? He groped in his pocket for a packet of gum and slid a stick into his mouth, then bit down hard to release the hot sting of cinnamon.

A slight smile hovered at the corners of the Gypsy's mouth. "He's at barn." She jerked her head toward the rear of the hotel.

A barn? Allan hadn't seen a barn from the parking lot but it could be behind the stand of trees shading the north side. He nodded his thanks as he pushed away from the counter. "I'll find it."

169

Her hand shot out, as if to stop him, then she let it fall. The dull look returned to her face.

He circled the hotel and found a path that sliced through the tree line. The remaining leaves on the trees shone a mix of copper and gold. The woman's reaction bothered him. Her expression had changed from triumph to fear. Why would she regret telling him where to find Misha?

The path skirted a pond and meadow before angling off to a rustic barn in the distance. It could be an attractive walk if he were with a group, but on his own, a sense of vulnerability set in. No sound from the village or the road reached this part of the property. He realized there was no sound at all--no bird song, no whisper of wind in the leaves, nothing.

The small hairs on the back of his neck rose as he thought again of the woman's reaction. She was a cowed woman, probably beaten by her husband. It wouldn't surprise him if Misha was into something illegal and his wife had intentionally told Allan where to find him out of spite -- to cause trouble -- then realized what she had done. She could pay big-time for her moment of power. Trouble was, if his suspicions were correct, Allan could pay big-time if Misha felt threatened by him. His steps slowed.

A sharp whistle split the air. Someone had been watching the path and passed on a warning to the barn. Fuck. What had he walked into? *Play it cool, man. Just play it cool.*

***

János had not exaggerated when he said the path to the second tunnel would not be an easy climb. The old

170

forester led the group, albeit slowly, as they worked their way around lichen-covered boulders and scraggly, sunscorched vegetation.

Stan noted that Sonja struggled to keep up as she climbed the steep slope along a path barely wide enough for a goat to negotiate. At one point, loose stones skittered away beneath their feet sending small slides of scree tumbling down the slope. It was then he realized Sonja was wearing sandals, rather than walking shoes. When they left the hotel this morning no one realized they would be making such a vigorous climb.

"You okay back there?" he called to her.

"So far, so good. But if I turn an ankle, you will be the one carrying me down."

They stopped to give János a chance to catch his breath. Stan hunkered down beside him, the gun he'd accepted from Feri heavy in his waistband. He was no expert in European weapons, but he thought it looked like a Makarov.

"I'm curious, Uncle. Where does the second tunnel start in the castle."

The old man frowned. "In dungeons. Many walls collapsed. Depending on ruling government party some make repairs to bring tourists. Tunnel is found during one repair. Then new government is not good so no tourists, no repairs. Tunnel forgotten by most people. Smugglers have fixed walls so some of dungeon can be used to store guns...drugs...people." He spit into the dirt. "They keep people in dungeons until they can be moved again. Same with guns."

The houses in the village weren't visible from this angle. Somewhere in the distance a dog barked, and as a breeze passed he caught the faint aroma of baking bread. If not for the information János had given him it would be

171

easy to imagine they were on an afternoon hike rather than searching out smuggled arms.

János got to his feet and they set out again.

Ten minutes later the old man crouched to examine animal droppings in the dirt. "Mule. Is not too old. Someone come to tunnel not too long ago." He signalled them to stay put as he scrabbled across the slope, moving from boulders to low outcroppings before Stan lost sight of him. In the silence he heard the sound of a logging truck shift gears. Were they that close to the road?

Several minutes later János reappeared, breathing hard, his face grim. He nodded. The tunnel was occupied.

Stan leaned against a rock outcropping as he scanned the area. The incline of the slope had eased a few degrees allowing the tree line to advance to within a few hundred metres of where they stood. It was the perfect place for the exit of an escape tunnel. But he'd need to have a look at the exit himself so he knew how to advise the contact.

"If the tunnel exit is lower than where we are, it could be almost at the tree line," Feri said. "Fairly easy access in and out through the trees--no houses on this side of the hill. It wouldn't be hard to get a mule up here, either."

"How far are we from the exit?" Stan asked János.

"Maybe 30 metres. It is around," he moved his hand to simulate the curvature of the hill, "then just down little bit." A dusty finger pointed to the general area of the exit. "Big bush grows beside rocks. Is easy to miss opening."

"Stan?" His wife's voice broke into his thoughts. "You're not going in there, are you...into the tunnel?" She clutched his arm.

He took her hands in his and tugged her into a crouch beside the rock. "You're going to stay here. Remember, you promised you'd do as I asked."

Her eyes travelled to the gun in his waistband.

"I'm not going in, Sonja. But I'd like to know exactly where the opening is, and if possible, what's going on in there."

"Then what?"

A good question. He would use the contact number, but only after he knew for certain what was happening inside. No use getting everyone excited if local kids had decided to take the day off school to party in the bowels of an old volcano. The dung that János had identified as mule droppings bothered him. There would be no reason for kids to bring mules up here. "We'll see." He stood.

Feri moved to his side. "I will go with you. Believe me, I'm pretty good at stuff like this."

173

CHAPTER THIRTY-ONE

They followed the route János had taken, watching for signs where the old man had dislodged rocks or made a mark in the scant soil. The large shrub was easy to find, but the light and dark shadings of the surrounding rock made the opening almost impossible to spot. If Stan hadn't known it was there, he would have missed it.

He turned to motion Feri to keep low, but his brother-in-law was already in a crouched position, working his way at a slight angle to approach the opening from the opposite side. He was good, as he had stated, but where had he acquired his expertise? Stan realized there were probably a few things about Feri he was better off not knowing. For Sonja's sake he had to accept her brother as he was now, not for what he had been in the past.

Stan crab-walked his way to the shrub that helped camouflage the opening from his angle. His hand rested on the butt of his gun, but the situation could turn to disaster if he got trigger-happy. It might be a couple of kids messing around inside, or locals using the tunnel to brew moonshine. He could think of a number of laws he was breaking by simply having the weapon in his possession. Better to wait until he knew he needed it.

The climb and tension had elevated his heart rate. He took several deep breaths and concentrated on slowing the pulse in his ears. His hearing needed to be as sharp as he could get it. If any movement occurred near the mouth of the tunnel he wanted to know about it before he stuck his head around the rocks.

When the sound of human activity came it wasn't from the opening in front of him. It carried from the forest below. A group of men worked its way through the trees. The clink of harnesses and loud laughter marked their passage, then the braying of a cranky mule, followed by curses.

Not kids then. Stan spared a moment to be grateful Sonja and János were safely out of sight beyond the curve of the hill, then concentrated on the forest below.

Feri hissed a warning and pointed at the opening. Stan ducked lower as he strained to hear. Silence. Then a whiff of cigarette smoke. Someone was waiting inside to receive the men when they arrived.

He had to move. Once the men left the trees they'd spot him. He motioned Feri back, then left the shelter of the shrub for a cleft above the opening. The space was tight and he could no longer see the tunnel opening, but he still had a clear view of the forest's edge. At least he'd know how many men were coming along the track and could get an idea of what they were smuggling. Anything he could add in his phone call would be a help.

The men left the cover of the forest, cursing and tugging the leads of five mules, three loaded with long wooden crates. Rifles, Stan guessed, or possibly RPGs. The other animals carried metal boxes of odd sizes--some square, some flat. Shells, grenades, handguns? Whatever the content of the boxes, it meant death to someone, somewhere. The men wore backpacks that appeared, from the way they moved, to weigh heavy on their shoulders.

Was Misha among them? Probably not. Stan couldn't see the innkeeper getting his hands dirty unloading weapons and leading mules. He'd be the one working behind the scenes.

A shout sounded from the lurker in the tunnel mouth. The lead man of the group answered as he climbed the slope. Harsh laughter moved down the line of men. They were close enough now that Stan could see their faces but Misha wasn't among them. Stan wasn't surprised. He looked at each man carefully. He wanted to be sure he could pick them out of a photo line-up.

Sharp hooves clicked against rock as the animals struggled up the grade. A commotion broke out at the tunnel opening. From the sounds of it one or more of the mules had balked. Although out of view, Stan could picture the scene below: panicked animals, crates crashing against stone walls, the sharp twisting of tails and several loud smacks on the rump. Whatever technique used the reluctant animals complied. Within minutes of the small cavalcade leaving the forest the hillside was once again empty and quiet.

He was about to leave the protection of the cleft when a now familiar sound caught his attention--the uneven catch of a diesel motor in need of a tune-up, the hydraulic shift of gears, the deepening growl as wheels caught on a gravel road. A fine line of dust filtered through the brightly coloured treetops before diminishing as the truck sped away. The arms shipment had arrived on a logging truck.

It was time to leave. He'd call Jim, report on what he'd found and get back to his original assignment. As he was about to push out of the fissure a small slide of stones near his hand stopped him. Someone had approached from above.

Shit! Another guard. He should have checked the area more carefully. His hand went to his waistband for the gun but there wasn't room to draw it free. He was trapped.

"It's me, my friend," Feri whispered. He slid from the overhanging rock and wiggled his slight frame into the narrow space beside Stan.

As the adrenaline rush drained from Stan's body he gripped his brother-in-law's shoulder and squeezed. "Do you know how-the-hell close you came to having a new navel?"

Feri's eyebrows drew together in question, then he glanced at Stan's hand on the weapon. "I have been close before. It's better we don't mention it to Panna or Sonja, okay?" He pointed to the scene below. "I was over to the left, there. I could see inside. Only one person was on guard when the men came up. I do not know how many could be further along the tunnel, or in the dungeon area. Perhaps none. From the size of the load I don't think they would need more men. What do you think?"

Stan had to agree. The more men that knew about a shipment, the more chances someone would talk. Also, fewer men meant a larger payout for services rendered. "Did you catch anything they said?"

He thrust out his lower lip and shrugged a shoulder. "A bit. They said everything went well. Someone complained about a new inspector from the forestry service being a dickhead as they crossed the border, but that's all. No word on whether Misha will be coming to inspect the load. I would think he will come."

Stan had seen enough. He needed to get away from the area, back to Sonja and János, back to where it was safe to make the phone call.

There was no way of knowing if a guard had been posted along the treeline so they kept low to the ground as they worked their way along the curve of the hill. No alarm sounded, but that didn't mean the smugglers didn't have the use of cell phones. He was fairly certain there was reception in the area, considering the elevation of the dome.

Sonja and János sat at the base of a large white

boulder, their eyes closed, enjoying the early afternoon sun on their faces. As Stan and Feri joined them Sonja glanced up but János did not. Stan frowned in concern but Sonja shook her head. "He's taking a power nap. He says it's good for stamina."

One eye opened under János's shaggy eyebrows. "I am awake. You cannot sneak up on old forester that easy. I was in business of staying alive before even you were born."

Feri grinned as he helped the old man to his feet. "You're still in the business of staying alive, Uncle. Lead us out of here on the quickest trail you can find. Stan has a phone call to make."

They followed the bulge of the dome to where the village was visible below before Stan felt it safe enough to stop. He scrolled the list of contacts on his phone then tapped the number to dial the mysterious Jim.

Two rings, then the connection was made.

"Jim, here."

The reception was perfect. Jim could be sitting in a restaurant in Ujhely for all Stan knew.

"Stan Boyko," he replied, "special assignment with the RCMP out of Winnipeg, Manitoba."

"Well greetings to a fellow Canuck. In fact, greetings to a fellow Manitoban. Small world, eh?"

The exhilaration that had carried Stan from the mouth of the tunnel died. He was speaking to someone in Canada who could do nothing to apprehend the men who had just brought a shipment of arms--and possibly nuclear material, into the tunnel at Fuzer. Disappointment hit hard. Given Misha's botched attempt on his life, Stan would have liked to put an end to the group's activities. He turned his face to the sky and breathed out hard as he watched a hawk ride the air currents over the castle dome.

He had no jurisdiction here. Why had he allowed himself
to think he could accomplish anything?

CHAPTER THIRTY-TWO

"We're aware of your situation, Stan," Jim said, breaking into his thoughts "and we're ready to step in. Has the shipment been delivered?"

Stan reigned in his disappointment. His initial reaction was born of personal experience. He needed to operate on a professional level. "It arrived about a half-hour ago. Escort is seven men, one more on the receiving end of the tunnel. Possibly more inside, but I can't confirm that." A thought hit him. "Jim, can you give me your location?"

"We're almost on top of you. I'm attached to a UN Special Forces Unit positioned at the Slovak border. We cleared several suspect logging trucks an hour ago. Can you give precise instructions on the location of the shipment? I've been waiting a long time to catch these guys in action."

The Slovak border. Five kilometres from Fuzer. The smugglers had mentioned a new inspector. That would teach him to assume when he should be thinking. As for giving instructions on the location of the shipment? Not a chance. They would have to approach from both ends of the tunnel at the same time. Jim and his unit couldn't swoop in and arrest the men without someone to guide them. And if any of the smugglers managed to escape from the first tunnel, they might be able to make their way to the *second* tunnel that started in the chapel. In reality, they needed to plug both entrances and both exits--four holes.

"Pretty tough to do. I hope you have a good contingent with you. Any chance we can meet at the parking lot at the foot of the rise to the castle? It's just on the edge of the village, set back in the trees. There's a couple of picnic tables there. "

"We know the spot. We'll be there in ten minutes." The line went dead.

***

Allan raised a hand in greeting as Misha stepped from the barn. "Good afternoon. Hadn't heard from you so thought I'd stop by and see if you'd found someone to help me out."

The Gypsy folded his arms across his chest. "I asked around. No one remembers your professor, Mr. Howland."

A second man wandered around the corner of the building to join him. The lookout? Both men wore surly looks.

It wouldn't do him any good, Allan realized, to back down now. He would only look guilty, like he'd come to snoop. He didn't give a rat's ass if Misha and his sidekick were screwing the maids or selling long-distance telephone cards out of the barn. That was their business. His business was his next pay cheque. He'd demanded a huge advance with the promise of an international story. If he didn't produce, the paper would fire his sorry ass.

He ploughed on. "Think I'll just head over to the lodge on my own then. I'll be careful." He turned to leave, then glanced back. "Oh, by the way. Met your Canadian visitors in town this morning. Him and his wife." As Allan expected, Misha reacted with interest.

"It is unfortunate," Misha said, "but they had an accident with a logging truck yesterday. They went to report it to the police."

"That right? Well, they didn't seem too upset.

181

Matter of fact, they were off to explore Fuzer today. Had a guide. Skinny fella--"

Misha barked an order in Hungarian at his partner, then turned to Allan. "I'm very busy. Good day to you, sir." He stepped into the barn and slammed the door.

Allan breathed a sigh of relief. He'd set something in motion--what exactly, he wasn't sure. The Canadian was up to something and that something was of huge interest to Misha.

He glanced at his watch--one o'clock. The cop had said they needed to be back in Ujhely at four to put someone on the train and check for emails. That meant three hours to waste. He may as well check out the hunting lodge. He started back up the path to the parking lot then stopped.

How could he be so stupid? If Misha was interested in what was happening at Fuzer then Fuzer was the place to be – not the lodge.

He limped back to the Mercedes and climbed in. He was thirsty and hungry. Hopefully, he could pick up something in the village. Sausage and a few buns would do. He'd take them to the picnic area in the parking lot while he took a load off his knees.

Misha reached for his cell phone as he slammed the barn door shut. Sipos had been right--again. The Canadian *was* here to investigate the shipments. The realization that his boss could out-think him made Misha's anger worse. "László," he bellowed at his helper. "Get the car."

Where was Boyko's back-up waiting? The cop wouldn't move in alone, not a chance! He would need help. Not the local police. The UN maybe? They had people crawling all over the Balkans. They could be

182

anywhere. He had to try to stop the shipment. Or cancel it.

Who would be driving the logging truck today? Stress made it hard to think properly. If he reached the truck before it made the turn onto the sidetrack behind Fuzer he could still rescue the deal. He flipped the cover of the phone. *Bassza meg!* No reception. The stinking tower probably wouldn't pick up the satellite until he reached Fuzer. No time to stop the shipment drop but maybe he could still make it in time to stop the transfer to the tunnels. If the cops were smart they'd allow the men and shipment to enter the tunnel before they made the seizure.

Who had talked? Who had accepted a bribe and then turned on him? He'd find the asshole and kill him.

Misha stuffed the phone into his pocket and made a mental note to get a new one soon. With today's technology, someone could probably find a lot of information on it that he didn't even realize was there. He grabbed two bottles of cheap wine and a portable stereo from the storage shelf. If he ran up against a road block or other group that smelled official around Fuzer he'd need a cover.

László pulled up in front of the barn in the battered Renault. Not much to look at, but Misha was proud of the impressive engine under the hood. He climbed in and slammed the door. "Drive! We're going to Fuzer. Take the back way that comes out on the secondary logging road. He reached into the door's side pocket, tugged out a squashed hat and pulled it onto his head.

As the vehicle tore out of the driveway to the main road Misha tipped a generous amount of wine over the stained seat and down his legs. He sloshed a mouthful before swallowing it. "Here," he shoved the bottle at the driver. "Take a mouthful. One only. Spit some onto your shirt. If we're stopped, we're out for an afternoon of fun."

They covered the half-hour trip to Radvany in twenty minutes. Fuzer was only fifteen minutes further. Misha cautioned László to back down to the speed limit. If the police pulled him over for drunk driving, Misha's problems would multiply. Normally no policeman would be stupid enough to bother him, but now -- now he didn't know who to trust. Someone had turned on him.

The side road around Fuzer was little more than a dirt track. As the Renault turned onto the narrow road Misha turned the dial on the stereo, then jacked up the volume. If they met anyone they were two drunks looking for a place to party. It would do for a cover.

CHAPTER THIRTY-THREE

A dusty troop carrier with canvas sides waited in the parking lot beside an SUV. Several men in fatigues and assault rifles had fanned out along the perimeter while one leaned, arms crossed, against the front bumper of the SUV. Stan had no trouble identifying the man as Jim. He looked like a typical Canadian. Brown hair, good strong build, a take-charge confident manner. Several days growth of beard provided a dark foil to solid white teeth when he smiled a greeting.

Stan eyed the rest of the group. Ten men in addition to the perimeter guards, a disparate assortment. One wore the uniform of the forestry service, several others were dressed as border guards, and two were in civilian clothes. Overall, they appeared well trained and alert even as they lounged around the troop carrier.

Given what they hoped to accomplish, they'd better have a good plan. Stan greeted his fellow countryman. "You have no idea how good it is to see you."

"Same here. Always nice to meet another Canadian, even in a tricky situation like this." He extended his hand; the grip was firm.

"I've got to ask--how the *hell* did you happen to be at the border when this shipment came through?"

Jim laughed. "I'm actually stationed in Kosovo." He reached through the vehicle window for a map lying on the seat. "We've followed several shipments back to this point on the Slovak border, then lost their trail. The locals are pretty tight lipped, and we weren't able to get anyone on the inside to loosen up. Then, fortunately or unfortunately depending on how you look at it, the last two shipments broke the ice and caused a bit of chatter.

Seems the purchaser agreed to transport a little something special along with his order to get the price lowered on his goods. Some of his men didn't take well to the idea. They had something to say about it to our undercover crew." He jerked his thumb toward the men in civvies.

Stan winced. He had a pretty good idea what the 'something special' might be. Feri and János joined them for introductions. When Stan glanced around for Sonja he located her at a picnic table near the back of the car park, head cradled in her arms, dozing. The trek around the dome had been tough.

As two of Jim's team removed equipment from the truck he spread the map over the hood of the SUV. "We knew the truck was coming and had one of our men, posing as a border guard, clear it at the Slovak border. After losing the other shipments we had a GPS unit ready to attach to the truck when it went through."

"Technology at its best, eh." Stan commented. "What went wrong?"

"What, indeed. Somewhere between the time we arrived and set up--and the time the truck appeared, someone fiddled with the unit. Disabled the guts. It looked fine to a casual glance but when my man went to attach it to the truck he noticed it felt light. Turns out the circuit boards were missing."

"One of your men?"

"I'd trust my men with my life. My bet's on one of the regular border guards. He's probably paid to turn a blind eye and figured he'd earn a little extra by disabling the GPS." Jim shrugged. "Well, it is what it is. Nothing we can do about it now." He leaned over the map and traced a route. "We have a spotter just outside Radvany. The truck made a half-hour stopover somewhere-- obviously to unload--so it broke off from the main road but we weren't sure where." He traced an area that included the mound of Fuzer castle. "This where they went?"

Feri translated the question to János. The older man leaned over the map and ran his finger along a faint line that circled behind the volcanic cone to indicate the route of the truck. His stubby digit halted at the western slope.

"At about this point," Stan said, "a path leads through the forest up the back-side to the old tunnel. They used mules to ferry the crates and boxes. But the opening is well hidden. Unless you're looking for it, you'll have trouble spotting it."

Jim straightened, his hands on his hips. "So that explains it. I left two more men at the border. I'll have them circle around back and locate the point where the goods were unloaded. Shouldn't be hard to find. From there it's a matter of tracking. Seven men and mules don't move over ground without leaving a trail."

He pulled his cell phone from a holder on his belt and punched in a number. Within minutes he had relayed concise instructions to the team at the border on how to reach the drop zone and cover the western tunnel exit. He snapped the phone shut. "They'll be there in ten minutes-- max."

Stan sighed in relief. With the extra men securing the tunnel exit, any plan Jim had in mind now seemed doable.

"Where does the tunnel begin? Inside the castle?" Jim asked.

"Right. In the dungeon area. It's off-limits to regular visitors. János says they've modified some of the cells, even erected temporary walls in case heritage inspectors nose around."

Jim ran the knuckles of one hand across the bristles on his chin as he considered the situation. "Damn! I wish

187

we had a floor plan of that castle. It would help if I knew what my men are in for once they get up there. "

A floor plan. Stan had seen one today, but where? At the arch over the drawbridge, or at the bottom of the trail leading up the cone? No, it was here in the lot somewhere. He did a quick 360 degree turn as he scanned the area. There, at the end of the first row of parking spaces--a wooden box nailed to a pole with a schematic of the castle secured to the top of the box by a sheet of plexiglass. He'd seen the same set-up at the head of cross-country ski trails in Canada. Inside the box would be a stack of photocopies of the map for visitors wanting a self-guided tour. Stan sprinted across the lot and returned with several copies of the schematic.

Jim's eyes widened as he reached for the papers. "Your middle name must be Genie. When this is over grant me another wish. I'd appreciate an airline ticket so my wife can visit for a while."

He placed the schematic on the table and studied it for several minutes. "Okay, this is how it will play out. We've got the one team already on their way around back to watch that exit. Our group will spread out across the castle's bailey--that's this yard area--and enter the dungeons here." His finger travelled across the diagram of the castle. "We'll have them bottled up. With both exits blocked they'd have to have a death wish to try and fight their way out."

But the smugglers might fight, Stan mused, because they knew there was another way off the castle mount. No time like the present to break the news to Jim about the second tunnel leading from the chapel.

The agent took the news in stride. "We'll have to have men in the chapel, but we won't need to cover the exit of that second tunnel if we contain the smugglers in the dungeon. So there's three exits to block. Agreed?"

Stan agreed. With limited manpower, it made sense to concentrate their efforts where it mattered most. If all went well, the smugglers would never make it to the chapel. They'd leave the dungeon in handcuffs.

A shout rose from the entrance to the parking lot. A Mercedes was trying to enter the area. *Where have I seen that car before?* Then he had it. The same vehicle passed through Radvany when they stopped to pick up Uncle János. He watched with interest as the driver exchanged words with the guard blocking the road.

The car began to back out of the lot, followed by the guard. Suddenly it stopped and a man stepped out, hands extended in the air. Another shout of warning from the guard cut the air as the man began to walk toward the parking lot.

"I know him," Feri hissed. "I recognize the walk. See how he limps. It's that damned reporter, Allan Howland! He's tight with Sipos."

Stan recognized the newcomer as well. The man had taken a seat beside them in the post office computer room that morning. Somehow Allan Howland had gotten wind of what was happening and followed them from Ujhely.

"What's up, Stan?" Jim said, "You know the guy?"

"No. Not personally. Feri knows him and isn't impressed with the company he keeps. Better keep an eye on him, and don't trust anything he says."

"Recommendation noted. The two of you best come with me."

As they approached Howland the reporter removed a press card from his wallet. Jim examined the worn document and returned it. "What business do you think you have here?"

"I've got some important information for you and the

189

Canadian cop." He thrust his chin in Stan's direction. "Considering what you're getting into, it would be best if you listened to what I have to say."

***

Allan made no attempt to hide his satisfaction. His instincts hadn't failed him. He turned to address Boyko, and his scrawny sidekick. "Afternoon, gentlemen. If you didn't know, my name's Allan Howland. But then I don't have to introduce myself to you, Feri, do I? We've met before, although it's been a while--and under vastly different circumstances." The ferret's discomfort provided a small measure of satisfaction.

Allan shoved his hands into his pockets to hide the tremors coursing through his fingers. Whatever he said in the next few minutes would make the difference between success or disaster. "I've got some information you'll find useful. Of course it comes at a price, but a small one. I would like an exclusive on the operation that's about to go down."

Boyko's eyebrows rose to meet his hairline. "And what would that be, exactly?"

Allan's mind raced through the information he had. Boyko was looking for something. He must have found it and called in his back-up because the idiot at the entrance to the parking lot had identified himself as *policija*. No matter what language he claimed as his mother tongue, *policija* meant 'police'. Then, on the walk across the lot he spotted the canvas-walled truck tucked into the back, a stack of baby-blue berets slumped on the running board next to a bullhorn. Sweet Jesus. He'd seen those berets before. The goons in the lot were with the UN. This was *big*.

190

Then there was Misha's reaction when Allan had mentioned Fuzer. He barely had time to leave the parking lot of Misha's hotel when the Gypsy and his cohort came tearing out a side road from the barn in a souped-up beater. A man didn't need to be a rocket scientist to realize they were headed to Fuzer. Something was going down at the castle mount and it wasn't working out the way Misha had planned.

Finally, there was the involvement of the UN. Two things the UN were interested in enough to launch a mini operation like this: drugs and guns.

Allan was willing to stake his future as a reporter that Misha wasn't hanging out in the barn to bang the maids or sell phone cards. He had a drug or gun-running operation at Fuzer and the UN had gotten wind of it. From the looks of it, they were about to make a raid.

Three things didn't fit with the scenario he'd worked out. One was the Canadian's interest in the hunting lodge. Two, the Carl McCartney connection. The third was the presence of Feri. The lodge could have been a lead that didn't pan out. And Feri? Maybe an uncover agent. Sweet Jesus! If Sipos only knew.

Whatever the details were, Allan had to take a chance he had enough worked out that he could bluff his way through.

He squared his shoulders and flashed a confident grin. "I know where Misha is right now. It'd be in your best interest to have that info or, as they say - the shit will hit the fan."

191

CHAPTER THIRTY-FOUR

Sonja woke with a crick in her neck and in urgent need of a bathroom. How long had she slept? Not long enough. Tiredness still clung to her, numbing her bones and clogging her mind. She'd been tired for a couple of weeks, but never like this. She's put the earlier tiredness down to jetlag, but now…. The climb and trek around the castle mound had really tired her out.

The odour as she opened the door of the picnic area's outhouse stirred nausea, but foul as it was it was a better option than squatting in the margins of the parking lot.

When they'd entered the lot earlier she'd hung back as Stan greeted the contact he'd talked to on the cell phone. Then the weariness hit her, and a nap on the picnic table seemed more important than an introduction. Stan told her they were meeting a team from the UN, yet the person he was talking to now didn't seem to fit the picture of a UN official. He stood, one hipped cocked, his arms crossed as he listened intently to what Stan was saying.

She didn't see Feri or Uncle János in the group then noticed them at the Skoda, leaning on the bumper, conducting their own meeting. Of course. The main conversation in the centre of the lot would be in English, a language neither understood. Should she join János and her brother, or Stan? Would she be intruding on official business if she joined her husband? Finally, curiosity got the best of her and she headed toward the main group in the centre of the lot.

"He'll probably try to reach the smugglers with a cell phone, but I doubt they'll get reception in the tunnel. I'm confident they don't…" The speaker broke off as she approached. Stan introduced her to Jim.

Someone with a limp walked over, waiting for an introduction but Stan ignored him. He stepped forward. "Allan Howland, reporter for the Chicago Courier. Nice to meet you."

"Sonja Boyko, I'm pleased--"

Her husband put his arm around her shoulders and drew her close, cutting short her reply. He didn't like the man. Why?

"Our new friend here," Stan gave Howland a nod, "has brought some interesting news about Misha. It's not good." Before he could continue, the phone on Jim's belt vibrated against the leather, silently alerting the owner to a phone call.

As Jim listened to the call the planes of his face hardened. "Detain him. And the other one, too. Assume they're armed. And don't let them make a phone call. Under *any* circumstances. We'll deal with the fall-out later. Have you spotted the tunnel exit?" He held Stan's gaze as he listened to the conversation on the other end. "Good, keep it covered. Anyone comes out, detain them, too."

He snapped the phone shut. "They've spotted Misha. He and the driver left a car about a kilometre down the road from the drop-off point. He's heading for the tunnel. That answers one question. If he knew we were here he wouldn't have taken a chance to reach his group. I'm confident the men in the dungeons have no idea they were spotted." Jim strode to the troop carrier and began to hand out blue berets.

Sonja tugged on Stan's elbow. "Tell me what's going on. What did I miss?"

Before he could answer a blue beret flew through the air in his direction. He caught it and stared at the hat, a look of surprise on his face.

193

"Prepare to move out," Jim yelled. One of his team snapped open a weapon box and distributed stubby assault rifles while a second removed vests from a crate near the wheels of the vehicle.

The appearance of the guns and the hat in Stan's hand sent a shock up Sonja's spine. "You're not going with them. Tell me you're not!"

"Sonja." He grasped her hand and lead her a short distance from the group. "Jim doesn't have a lot of men. You know how many there are up there. Plus, they can't just saunter up the trail and wander into the castle's bailey. The smugglers may have a look-out posted. They need a guide."

"This isn't your job. We're here to find the papers--"

"I'm a member of the RCMP, Sonja. I'm a police officer, just like Jim. He needs help and I'm here."

She wanted to shake him, to slap him, to hug him and never let him go. At the same time, she realized he was right. From the moment he received the email in Ujhely he became part of Jim's team.

She clenched her hands into fists. "If you're not going up the main trail how are you going to get up there?" The answer hit her even as the words left her mouth. "The second tunnel. You're going to back-track through the second tunnel and come out in the chapel, aren't you?"

He nodded. "They'll need someone to lead them to the opening in the hillside behind the village."

Sonja shot a glance at Uncle János and Feri, then averted her eyes in guilt. No one expected the old man to make a second trip up the slope. He'd done well to make the first climb. "And Feri? What's Feri going to do?"

"I'd prefer to see him take you and János back to Radvany. Panna will be right and truly pissed off by now." He smiled. "We told her we'd be back around 1:00 o'clock and it's almost 3:00."

The smile did nothing to ease her fear. She drew back. "Absolutely no way! I'm not leaving here without you. I don't care what Feri does but I'm staying here. I'll...I'll stay with the reporter."

"Okay, stay." He held up his hands in surrender. "But here's what we'll do. I'll leave you my cell phone."

She snatched the phone, still warm from his hand, and hugged it to her chest. It was a link to him.

He took her by the elbow and led her toward the Skoda. "You won't be able to call me, but I can borrow Jim's phone to contact you."

Feri stood as they approached. "I'll go with you Stan, if you wish."

Sonja wanted to scream *No, not you too*, but Stan shook his head. "Thanks, Feri, but you're a civilian. And there's three more civilians here who need protection." He handed Feri's gun back to him. "You probably won't need it--but just in case. Uncle János has his knife and Jim's leaving two armed guards here. One to stop anyone from entering the parking lot, and one at the bottom of the trail to make sure no wandering tourists decide to end their day with a tour of the castle."

Uncle János stepped forward. "Stan, how do you know there is no guard in chapel? If you come out of tunnel and someone is in chapel you have big problem."

"Jim's on top of it. Two of his men, Viktor and Javor, were posing as civilians and aren't in uniform. They'll act as tourists and take the regular path to the castle. If someone's on guard and sees tourists, they'll draw back. If they have someone posted in the chapel..." There was no need to finish the sentence.

Sonja rushed to the picnic table where she'd left her

195

camera. "Here. They can take this. It will help them look more like tourists if they're carrying a camera."

***

Misha eased the car door shut. No use making more noise than necessary. He passed one of the bottles to László and swung the cumbersome stereo unit onto his shoulder. They'd go into the drunk Gypsy routine if they met someone.

The transfer spot for the shipment was a little over a kilometre up the road. If they cut into the forest here, they could approach the area at an angle. Best to stick to the trees until they were sure there hadn't been trouble during the transfer from the truck to the mules.

He should have called Sipos. The man liked to keep his finger on the pulse of all his operations. And he seemed to have a special interest in this shipment. Misha had probed a bit but met a stone wall.

A gust of wind sucked dried leaves from the trees, scattering the harvest in a noisy cascade. Branches snapped underfoot. Autumn wasn't the season to try and move through a forest without making noise. A rustle came from his right. An animal perhaps? Deer and boar were thick in this forest. His tension amplified the faintest noises. Behind him, the wheeze of László's nasal breathing sounded more like an asthma attack then the result of a broken nose.

He'd aimed too high and they came out on the trail to the tunnel exit. He didn't need to stoop to see that the sharp hooves of the mules and the passage of sturdy boots had beaten the earth on the track. Good. They had transferred the shipment. Everything seemed in order. He'd call Sipos and confirm the hand-over then try to reach his men.

He turned to hand László the bottle of wine and found himself staring into the barrel of a gun. The man on the other end of the weapon wore the blue beret of the UN.

CHAPTER THIRTY-FIVE

They worked their way through the thick border of trees around the parking lot then skirted the village, keeping well out of sight of prying eyes. Chances were good that someone in the small collection of houses knew about the smuggling activity at the castle but were sympathetic to the idea of supplementing income by moving contraband.

As they cleared the final house Stan led the way up the steep slope, searching for markers he had noted on his way down earlier in the afternoon. An odd shaped rock, a gap in a ridge, a hummock or angle of a scraggly shrub. The angle of the sun had moved enough to change the patterns on the basalt. Areas of rock that had been light earlier were now dark, altering the appearance dramatically. Plus, they were approaching from a different direction. Would he recognize the mouth of the exit? The opening they had crawled out of was small, but he remembered the massive, pale stones that surrounded it.

Ten minutes into the climb he realized they were too low. He'd allowed himself to be lured on the lower course by the ease of footing. It was hard going to work their way back up the slope but the men took the change of course in stride. As he skirted an outcropping of rock that resembled a blacksmith's anvil he glanced down to the treeline. He'd got them back on track. In the distance he recognized the edge of a harvested field shining pale gold in the afternoon sunlight. Now, to locate the opening.

Jim moved forward to join him. "I've just received word that they have Misha and a second man in custody.

He's screaming for a phone call, but my men are stalling him. It wouldn't fly in Canada," he shrugged, "but this is Hungary. They're taking him to the lock-up in Szephalom. We can stall him for a few hours. How much further?"

"It's right around here. When we came out I remember seeing--hold on." Stan scrambled up the slope to the base of a group of boulders. Thank God. He'd found it.

While Stan explained what they would find on the other side of the entrance the men checked their weapons. "It's rock, so sound echos--bounces around. If someone is waiting in the chapel with the opening exposed, they'll know we're coming. Have you heard anything from the men who went up the tourist path?"

Jim glanced at the phone on his belt and shook his head. "Nothing. They'll have to do the tourist thing once they're up there. Nose around a bit, kick a few stones. Thanks to your wife's camera they can snap a couple of photos. We'll give them a few more minutes."

He passed around the schematic of the castle and traced the path they would follow to the dungeons once they were out of the chapel. "The forester, János, says there're about eleven steps down from ground level to the first landing in the dungeons. There're a few cells for prisoners at that point, then the false wall. The guns and the men are in the cells behind the wall. Adimir," he nodded to one of the men, "since you're carrying the bullhorn I want you to keep to the back."

His phone hummed. Jim glanced at the text message and nodded. "It's Javor. They've secured their area. We're good to go."

Stan tested the small flashlight he'd borrowed from Uncle János. The beam seemed strong. He entered the tunnel first, the light gripped between his teeth. The men passed their weapons to him through the opening then followed on their hands and knees. Once inside they hugged the wall as Stan wove the beam across the floor. They moved along the stone passage with little sound, save for the rustle of litter on the floor.

Stan mentally reviewed Jim's plan and could find no flaw. Once out of the chapel they would fan out across the castle's bailey using the crumbling service buildings for cover as they made their way to the dungeon entrance. The bakery, stables and blacksmith sheds were ruined shells but could still provide protection if they needed it. The real challenge would come once they entered the door to the dungeon.

A narrow wedge of light ahead signalled the approach of the end of the tunnel. Viktor or Javor had moved the pillar of the altar stone– He stopped so suddenly the man behind him trod on his heels. *How did they know about the pillar?* Stan had not thought to mention it.

He cut the beam of the flashlight. Spreading his arms wide he stepped back, forcing the men behind back with him. They were well trained; no one commented on his abrupt actions.

After several steps he turned and whispered. "Jim-- could be trouble. Someone opened the entrance." The smugglers might have overpowered Jim's men. He, and the six with him, could be walking into a trap.

***

Vexed, Sonja crossed her arms as she watched Stan's group melt into the treeline surrounding the parking lot. Across the road, Viktor and Javor lingered to give the

200

tunnel team a head start before they began their own steep climb up the path that led through the arch to the castle bailey. She glanced at Feri and Uncle János. Neither seemed pleased with their forced inaction, nor did the reporter. What was his name? She'd forgotten.

He removed a briefcase and a paper bag from the trunk of his car. At a picnic table he set about scribbling notes on a yellow pad of paper while cramming an improvised lunch of sausage and buns into his mouth. A big man with a big appetite. He probably had a big appetite for everything in life, not only food but drink, women, his career. He'd managed to figure out what they were up to here. How?

Sonja eyed the food. Her stomach reacted with first a growl of hunger quickly followed by a rush of nausea. He could keep his food for all she cared but he could have offered to share it with the others.

Feri interrupted her thoughts. "If I can borrow Stan's phone, I'll call Panna. She will be worried. Even though they have Misha in custody, I don't want her trying to call us at the hotel." He chuckled. "I guess she won't be using that train ticket after all."

Sonja smiled as she listened to her brother sooth his wife without explaining why they were so late returning to Aunt Anna's. They seemed happy together as a couple. The baby was a real sweetie. One day she and Stan would have– *Oh, my God! Of course. Why didn't I realize before? I'm pregnant.* The nausea, the weariness, her tender breasts. She'd thought the travelling had put her off her cycle, but this made more sense. She retreated to the nearest picnic table to process the idea.

Mixed with joy was the realization that in a few months life would change forever. No more impromptu outings, no more romantic getaways. The focus of their life would be a child and the needs of a family rather than the spontaneous desires of two carefree people. She thought of Panna, spending the afternoon with Aunt Anna while Feri, Stan and she raced around the countryside rooting out smugglers with the UN. With her background, she'd never taken her independence for granted, but once gained she had never thought of losing it, either.

A baby! We're going to have a baby. She hugged herself tightly to savour the discomfort the action brought. Whatever constraints having a child might bring they were worth it, ten-fold. She still had about seven months. She could pack a lot into that time. Starting right now.

"Feri," she called to him, "do you think Jim and Stan will be able to open the entrance to the chapel from inside the tunnel?"

He slouched over to her, his hands deep in his pockets. "I doubt it. The people who constructed it wouldn't have wanted the enemy to come in that way. I suspect the only way to open it is from the chapel side."

"Do Viktor or Javor know how to open it?"

His eyes lit with a gleam of understanding. "I don't think anyone mentioned it to them."

Sonja stood. "That's what I thought. This castle needs a few more tourists, don't you think? Someone who knows how to move an altar stone."

CHAPTER THIRTY-SIX

Sonja grabbed a map from the box as they crossed the road. Without her camera she wanted something to help them look touristy. "Hurry. We should catch up to Viktor and Javor."

The pseudo-tourists were taking their time as they made the climb, stopping occasionally to admire the view or point out landmarks. For the benefit of anyone watching from above, as Sonja and Feri got within hailing distance she called a cheerful greeting. She doubted they would order her back once she explained her reason for joining them. They surprised her.

"You can explain to us how to open the tunnel entrance, then you must go back to the parking lot."

"So, if I explain it to you and you send us back," Sonja gestured up the path, "what does it look like from up there? What if someone is watching? They will be on edge anyway. It will look suspicious."

They conceded her point, but neither man looked happy as they continued to climb as a foursome.

Although Sonja knew seven smugglers were in the castle, the courtyard appeared empty as they entered through the arch. No lounging men, no flitting shadows on the edge of her vision. But what about out of her range of vision? There were endless places people could hide.

She worked at calming her imagination. If she wanted to be a help she had to stay in control. The men in the dungeons were smugglers, not psychopaths. With that thought, the tension in her stomach eased slightly.

For the sake of their role as tourists they wandered the bailey. She asked for her camera back and snapped a few photos. Through the viewfinder every twig became a gun, every shadow a lurking danger.

Unlike earlier in the afternoon, she consulted the schematic and made special note of the placement of the ruined buildings. A missing door caught her attention. According to the diagram, there should be a door on the entrance to the dungeon; the door was no longer there. Would it be an asset or a problem when Jim's group made their assault?

When Javor and Viktor broke away Feri placed his hand on her arm to keep her at his side. "They're going into the chapel. They don't want you in there--in case someone is on guard." He directed her steps to the north wall and, for the second time that day, pointed out the nearby border. She reined in her anxiety as she dutifully admired a view that no longer captivated her.

Two minutes dragged into three, then four. If the chapel was empty the men would have given a signal that all was well. Sonja gripped the stone rampart as she pretended to admire the lancet windows of the tower. The skin between her shoulder blades twitched. "Something's wrong. Why aren't they coming for us? They don't know how to open the tunnel. They need us in there."

She turned from the wall and absently tossed a pebble at a twisted mass of shrubs struggling for existence in a right angle of tumbled rubble. The shrubs exploded in a flurry of harsh cries as a small flock of birds took flight, their protests echoing off the rough stone of the remaining walls. Sonja's hands flew to her mouth to muffle her answering cry of alarm.

Feri gripped her shoulder with one hand, the other stole to the gun under this jacket. "We'll give them a little longer." He let his arm slide to her waist and eased her toward the wall of what used to be the bakery. "I suspect there was a guard posted in the chapel."

Several more minutes crawled by, then Viktor appeared at the door of the chapel his hand raised to get their attention. "Hey. Come see in here," he called. "It's interesting." Sonja controlled her impulse to sprint across the courtyard in response to the invitation. Eyes could be watching from any number of hiding places.

***

Hands shoved Stan to the back of the group as Jim's men flattened themselves against the hewn rock of the tunnel wall. Fabric whispered as guns were raised. The rough scraping of rock against rock echoed in the tunnel followed by a slab of light bisecting the darkness ahead. The entrance had been opened wider. Breathing became louder as the men saturated their lungs with oxygen. Then a new sound reached his ears.

"Hello, Stan? Are you in there?" Sonja's voice, tense but clear, echoed off the walls.

What the hell? How did she get here? Stan's breath escaped in a small explosion.

At Jim's whispered command gun barrels dipped. Still cautious, the men crept forward. One bent, picked up a pebble from the ground and tossed it toward the light.

In response, a male voice called, "The room is secured, Jim."

Stan followed the team into the gloom of the chapel. A young man, no more than eighteen or nineteen, sat on the floor, knees drawn up to his chest, his hands cuffed behind his back. Javor hovered over him, a gun pointed at his head. Sonja stood to one side, clasping and unclasping her hands. She moved to greet him, then drew back.

205

"We were in the neighbourhood so Feri and I, we thought we'd--"

"In the neighbourhood? Christ! Sonja!" He grabbed her and held her close for a moment, then released her. "I asked you to stay with János!" He should have sent them all back to Radvany. Had the reporter come with them, as well?

Sonja pointed to the altar stone. "The way to open the tunnel. They didn't know how to do it. We were worried... maybe it couldn't be opened from the other side."

Jim stepped into the tunnel and signalled one of his men to move the altar stone into place. When the stone didn't move again after several minutes they pushed the pillar aside. Jim stepped out. "She's right. There's no way it could be opened from the inside." He nodded at the boy on the floor. "What's he have to say for himself?"

As the men crowded around the huddled figure Stan pulled Sonja to his side. With a finger under her chin, he tipped her face to his and pecked her on the lips. "I apologize. How did I ever find such a brave, stubborn, strong-willed woman?"

"And I love you too." She grinned. "I'll have you know you left out an adjective in describing me." She turned her attention to the group in the chapel.

It was a cryptic remark, but Stan had no time to dwell on it.

The young man cowered on the floor, his eyes darting from face to face to guns then back to faces. Stan had seen that look before--the young smuggler was on the verge of a panic attack. Fear squeezed the air out of his lungs no matter how hard he tried to draw it in.

Feri appeared at Stan's side. Good, he needed his brother-in-law's language skills. "I can't understand a thing they're saying. Can you make some sense out of it for me?"

Feri translated as the kid shook his head and at first denied any knowledge of smuggling, or of being a guard. As the questioning continued he finally admitted to being a guard but he didn't know what the men were transporting. Javor took over as inquisitor and changed the focus of the questions.

Feri continued to translate. "His father is there, with the guns, and an uncle. Six men in total. They are supposed to wait until dark, then someone will come and give them instructions."

Javor fired several more questions at the boy.

"He says he's only here because no one wants to work for the boss anymore. They couldn't find enough men to handle this shipment. The men that did come are unhappy about something but he doesn't know what it is. His father told him to leave, to come to the chapel, and stand guard. When he left, his father and the other men were arguing about something."

Finally, the boy could offer no more information. When the questions stopped he leaned his forehead against his knees. His sobs made it difficult for Stan to hear his final words. Feri turned his back on the scene. As he translated the words his tone betrayed his feelings of sadness. "He only came along because he wanted enough money to buy a train ticket to Budapest. He wanted to find real work so he could afford to buy his girlfriend an engagement ring."

Jim cleared his throat as he joined them. "I don't think there'll be too much resistance. We'll let them know we have the boy, and that Misha's in custody. They seem a pretty dispirited lot as it is."

Stan agreed. Had they somehow come to the

realization that nuclear material could have been added to the last few shipments? Whatever the reason was, the men had lost their stomach for what they were doing. Smuggling might be justifiable, but transporting mass annihilation was a totally different ball game.

CHAPTER THIRTY-SEVEN

"I'll have to ask you to stay here," Jim stated as he passed Stan a handgun. "The kid should behave, but you never know."

Stan accepted the Glock, the weight of it foreign in his hand. He glanced at the young smuggler. Someone had moved him against a wall so he had support for his back, his feet splayed in front of him. A cleared path in the grime on the floor testified that the men had dragged him, rather than allowing him to walk. He seemed somewhat calmer. Stan agreed that he wouldn't cause a problem. Even if he tried to shout a warning to the men in the dungeon the sound wouldn't carry past the walls of the chapel.

When the guard at the chapel door signalled all was clear in the bailey the team moved out. Sonja hunkered below his elbow to claim her view through the partially open door. There wasn't much to see. The men dispersed across the yard, merging with the elongated shadows created by the lowering sun on broken walls and rogue shrubs. Then the group was gone from view.

Stan kept his ears trained to any outside sounds as they waited. The boy conversed in muted tones with Feri, short anxious bursts followed by long pauses.

Suddenly a barked command in Hungarian shattered the quiet tension. The UN team had reached the dungeons and was using the bullhorn to communicate with the men inside. Stan itched to leave the chapel. If he followed the path the men had taken, used the crumbled walls for cover, and stopped short of the dungeon entrance, he could watch from there.

Tempting, certainly, but not responsible. He'd been

given a weapon by a senior officer and asked to guard the boy. He'd best stay put. Feri's gun had stayed out of sight. Stan could only speculate why he hadn't drawn it earlier.

Several minutes passed in strained silence. The boy stirred. His gaze met Stan's, a plea burning in their depths. A plea for what? For Stan to make the bad things disappear? His mother hadn't given birth to him for his role at this time in this place. His father had brought him here, true, but not for this outcome. Choices. Misha's choices, Feri's choices, the boy's choices. We all made them and once made they were bought and paid for. Trouble was, human nature seldom left room for the worst-case scenario.

Another command from the bullhorn. Silence. Then a single shot cut the air. Beside him, Sonja yelped.

"This may not be going so well," Feri murmured.

"Just a warning. To show they mean business," Stan replied. "They've got assault rifles, but that one wasn't set on automatic."

Boots thudded on the cobbles and the chapel door opened. A soldier from the unit issued an order. As Feri translated he helped the boy to his feet. "The kid's father wants to speak with him. If he is okay, they will come out. This mess is just about over, thank God."

***

Allan finished his notes with a flourish. Five pages. What a day, and it wasn't over yet. Not by far. If he worked the story right a news service might pick it up for syndication. His name would be on a by-line again. Hell, he might get a series out of it. Why not? He could walk the reader through the context--Sipos' parties, the reason the Canadian cop was in Hungary, the living conditions that made this area ripe for smuggling, that kind of thing. Readers would lap it up. He'd make it a 'Journey Through Hungary's Underbelly' theme.

Something scurried in his mind--not quite fully developed and just out of reach. Something didn't make sense. What about the McCartney connection? At the party Jordan, the Canadian Ambassador's secretary, said the cop had been asked to check out something to do with the Second World War and the royal family. Misha mentioned Stan seemed interested in the chateau. What was going on here? Were they just setting up a smokescreen?

Allan tapped the end of his pen against the pad of paper as he puzzled it through. The old man, János, might know, if they could speak to each other. Damned Hungarian gobbledy-gook!

And Sonja had said something interesting to her husband just before he left to take those UN yahoos on their jaunt up the mountain. Something about being here "to find the papers". Yes, that was it. Papers, not guns. The chateau had to do with spies, not smugglers. Ahh, this was getting, as little Alice said, "curiouser and curiouser". A sound, perhaps a gunshot, reached him. The old man rose from his seat at a picnic table and strode to the end of the parking lot. For such an old codger he carried himself well. Allan followed at a slower pace.

The guard had only a rudimentary command of English. He shrugged when Allan queried him. The shot could have come from the castle, or it could be a hunter. Hunting season was in full swing.

Allan returned to his pen and pad. Best to get everything down on paper, that's when it made the most sense.

Twenty minutes later János shouted for his attention and pointed to the castle. A knot of people made their way through the gate and began to descend the path. Allan suppressed a cry of triumph. He had his exclusive, but better yet, something more had to be going on here. *Chicago, your native son is gonna' make you proud!*

As the group worked its way slowly down the hill word spread in the village. Singly, and in small groups, people gathered at the foot of the path. Allan and János joined them to watch the sad procession descend.

Armed men in blue berets surrounded seven men in the middle of the group who stumbled awkwardly on the steep incline. As they neared the bottom Allan realized each unarmed man had his hands cuffed behind his back. Wails rose from the clutch of villagers. One woman grabbed a child and held the little boy's face in the folds of her skirt. A local must be among the group being escorted to the transport truck in the parking lot under the watchful eye of armed guards.

He'd have to try and interview them--at least one of them. "Are you taking them to Szephalom?" he called to a guard.

"Jail not big enough there. Just two cells. We take them to Ujhely."

So he'd have to go back to Ujhely. No matter, Allan reasoned. His things were still there at the hotel, anyway. Still, it would have been nice if they'd been kept locally.

He rubbed his hands together as he joined the Canadians, Feri the ferret, and János. "So then, on the chateau?" Four pairs of startled eyes swivelled in his direction. Bingo! Right, again. Fate was just pouring her good fortune on him today. A sweet libation.

"I beg your pardon?" Stan asked, his tone dark, menacing.

212

Allan faltered for a beat, then collected himself. "Thought we might cover some of the details about breaking the smuggling ring on our way to the chateau. You know, those World War Two papers. Carl McCartney. That stuff."

Stan stepped in close, to a point where he invaded Allan's personal space. "Mr. Howland. I'm not sure what you feel you know about any papers that may, or may not exist at a chateau. I can tell you, however, that unless you drop any investigating along those lines you will not get an exclusive, or even an explanation, of what happened here today. In fact, I can also suggest that you have very little chance of having another article published in any newspaper in North America or England at any time in the future. Do I make myself clear, sir?"

"What the hell you trying to pull? Some kind of cover-up? I'm just doing my job here. Hey! Hey, I'm talking to you!"

The cop had already turned to lead his wife toward the Skoda at the end of the lot.

"It won't work, Boyko," he yelled at their backs. "This story has legs and its going to take off, with or without you."

Allan's hands shook so badly he had trouble gathering his notes from the picnic table. Who the hell did the son-of-a-bitch think he was, talking to a member of the press like that? If Boyko had to resort to a threat those papers were a really big deal. Well, Mr. RCMP-man, it wasn't going to work. Allan Howland was going to get a piece of that action!

He needed a drink. How had he expected he could function without booze? Alcohol took the edge off. Kept him sharp. He flung his briefcase into the back seat of the Mercedes.

Either today or tomorrow they'd go to the chateau to get those papers. His money was on tomorrow. Still, to be on the safe side, he'd best camp out there in the car for a couple of hours tonight --until the light faded.

Trouble was, Boyko wouldn't share the information. He'd made that clear. Allan needed a way to force it out of him. Everyone had a weak spot. What was the cop's? How could he find out? Who would know? Jordan at the embassy? No, she'd given him everything she knew. Sipos! Sipos, might know something. Allan reached for his cell phone.

Given Feri's presence, Sipos might even have a stake in what had gone down today and would be grateful for the heads-up on the arrests. From what Allan had seen, Feri was either a mole in Sipos' organization or had changed sides. Yes, Sipos should be grateful enough to exchange information on the cop for what Allan knew. It was just a matter of playing his cards right.

CHAPTER THIRTY-EIGHT

"I felt sorry for him, Stan. He turned so pale!"

Stan reached for his wife's hand and gave it a gentle squeeze. He hadn't enjoyed being heavy-handed with Howland any more than she had enjoyed watching the duel of wills. "I had no choice. I didn't want him showing up at the chateau. The last thing anyone needs is a newspaper story on something that is supposed to be kept under wraps. I did what I needed to do for my assignment."

"Well, after you spoke to him like that I don't suppose he'll show his face again."

She pulled a bottle of water from the seat pocket in front of her and drank deeply. Fatigue showed in her eyes and the corners of her mouth. The day seemed especially hard on her.

Feri slowed the car for a curve before glancing back at them. "Should we go straight to Ujhely to check your email, or stop at Aunt Anna's? I know both she and Panna are worried about what we're up to. They suspect something."

Uncle János grunted in agreement. "Anna, she will be unhappy if she is kept in dark. Unhappy woman does not make good meal. I need good supper tonight." He patted the respectable mound of his midriff.

Stan joined the others as laughter filled the car. Muscles eased that he hadn't realized were taut. "I agree. Wherever those papers are they've been there for seventy years. We can wait until tomorrow to look for them. I've had enough excitement for one day. Maybe I can get the information I need over the phone, even if it's a diagram. That will save us having to go into Ujhely. It's worth a try."

Sonja scooted across the seat to snuggle against him. "I agree, too." She tried but failed, to suppress a yawn. "I'm...what is that you say, Stan? Dog-tired?"

He frowned as he stroked her hair. If they could get some private time alone tonight he'd have a talk with her. Something didn't seem right.

**

Sipos lunged from his chair and flung his cell phone against the wall. The action did little to relieve his anger, especially when the instrument of bad news remained in one piece. It would ring again, and again, each time bringing more bad news. Such things happened in threes. He had seen it before.

A pinpoint of white-hot rage ignited in his brain as he reviewed the reporter's words. The fury grew, fanned by the knowledge one of his former employees had betrayed him. He should have killed Feri when the spineless bastard slunk off to shack up with that dancer. Letting him live had been a moment of weakness on Sipos' part, one he would not repeat.

For months after Feri left the organization, Sipos expected to hear the Ukrainian had turned up in a gutter, like trash, pumped full of the drugs he had gotten hooked on. It hadn't happened. Then Feri dropped off everyone's radar. Sipos hadn't given him a thought in over a year. Well, he was back now, and somewhere along the line he'd grown a spine.

He'd made a mistake with Feri, Sipos reasoned, but he could fix it. Feri would die.

A spatter of rain driven by a cold September wind lashed the window in his office. He hated weather like

216

this. The moody, isolating drizzle chilled the bone and stirred up memories he'd sooner forget. His grandmother's sickness began with weather like this. If he'd had the money he did now, he could have saved her. Wave enough money in front of a doctor and they'd treat anyone, even a Gypsy. He turned away from the window. His useless memories would not help him today.

His foot struck the cell phone sending it in a looping trajectory across the hardwood floor. Bending, he scooped it up. He had to deal with Misha and with Feri. Then there was Feri's sister, Sonja. How had she managed to marry a Canadian cop? No, not a cop--a member of the Royal Canadian Mounted Police. Those bastards were tight with Canada's intelligence service.

Sipos remembered the girl. Good figure--amazing eyes. He'd had plans for her but she'd surprised him. She had too much spunk. Girls like that could be a problem. If you couldn't break them you'd end up killing them before they tried to kill you. Selling Sonja to the Canadian recruiter should have been the end of her, but, like her brother, she'd turned up again and screwed up his plans. Big time.

How much had he lost on the arms deal? Too much, but it paled in comparison to the consequences of losing the other part of the shipment. His mouth went dry at the thought. He needed a drink.

At the bar, he fixed a scotch and soda as he thumbed through his contact list on the phone. Who did he have in the Szephalom area? Someone would have to take care of Misha permanently. That was a given. If they offered Misha a deal in exchange for information there was no question what his choice would be. Misha had to go and Feri had to go. Why not make it three? Things happened in threes, didn't they? Maybe that's why the logging truck accident had failed. He'd only planned for two to die. Sonja had defied him and she had brought that cop over here to ruin his business. Spiteful bitch. Yes, she would be number three.

His finger paused on the phone's scroll button as it highlighted a name. Yes, there was someone he could count on to do the job properly. Nikola Kosma. The perfect man for this problem.

Thanks to the reporter, Sipos knew where to find Misha. It would be easy to send Nikola to the police station. The chief of police had earned a piss pot of money for turning a blind eye in the past. He could damned-well do it again while Misha got his payment.

Feri and Sonja-- now where would they be tomorrow? Nikola would have to find them himself. Sipos did a mental shrug. The man would have to be creative.

***

Despite János anticipation, the meal was a gloomy affair. Word of Misha's arrest had reached Aunt Anna and Panna before the Skoda pulled up to the Telkes home. The older woman wiped tears from her cheeks as she served a supper of leftovers. Misha was family, even though he'd gone down the wrong path in life.

"I can't believe you were going to send me home," Panna scolded as she spooned mashed potatoes into Eva's gaping mouth. "I won't be left behind when you go to the chateau, I can guarantee that."

A cell phone rang. Through his weary fog it took a moment for Stan to recognize the ring tone as his. Uncle János had arranged for sleeping accommodations in the village for all of them. As crowded or uncomfortable as

218

they may be, it would be better than returning to Misha's hotel. Thoughts of crawling into bed and curling up next to Sonja had held his attention for most of the meal.

It was Mark Willis, in Winnipeg. "We hear good news through CSIS. You did well, Stan. The department extends its thanks."

"No problem. My part didn't amount to much more than playing tour guide. Jim and his team did the work." He laughed. "We raise good RCMP officers in Manitoba, don't we? Any luck on that page from the chess book?"

"Absolutely. It was a diagram, just as you suspected. I sent a copy to your email address."

"Any chance you can explain it to me? Could save us a trip to another town."

"Sure, I have the original here." The sound of paper being shuffled filled the phone line, then Mark returned. "The caption said it's the deciding move of a game between Alekhine and Euwe held in The Hague in 1937. Alekhine became the first man in history to regain the World Chess Champion title."

Stan groaned. He'd need a chess expert or a book of chess moves. "Thanks, Mark. Hopefully, we'll have this wrapped up by tomorrow. I'll keep you informed."

He disconnected the call and turned to János. "Is there someone in the village who plays a lot of chess? I need a book of famous chess moves."

"Yah, yah. Putyi, he plays chess all the time." He spoke with Aunt Anna for a moment. She nodded and headed for the door. "She will ask Putyi to come with books tomorrow morning."

CHAPTER THIRTY-NINE

Dávid Vajda crooned into the phone in an effort to soothe his troubled sweetheart. "Bianka, I'm sorry I can't be there. I know I promised, but I swear someone gave me the evil eye. Both my commanding officer and the other deputy booked off sick this morning."

He listened as Bianka told him what his commanding officer could do with himself. The action was something Dávid agreed with wholeheartedly but could never hope to express in his superior's company.

"Yes, I'm sure there is a regulation about more than one person being on duty with a prisoner, but what can we do about it? Szephalom is a small community. There are only the three of us. I promise--I'll be over tonight."

Visions of Bianka's firm breasts and round hips filled his head for the next twenty minutes as he tidied the small police station's office. The day couldn't end soon enough.

When the squat man strode into the station the hairs on the back of Dávid's neck stood at attention. If the rumours were true and Misha had led the smuggling ring, then it was no surprise Nikola Kosma wanted to see him. Nikola had a bad reputation. In the young duty officer's opinion, Kosma had only served a fraction of the time he had coming to him.

Dávid's gut tensed as Nikola moved to the counter.

"I want to speak with Misha."

"He has a visitor already. He's only allowed one at a time." Dávid checked the large clock on the wall. Where was the old woman who brought breakfast when they had a prisoner? She had been contacted the night before and told her services were needed this morning. He would feel better with someone else in the building. He'd probably made a mistake letting that reporter see Misha. The man looked like he'd been up all night and he reeked of booze. He'd flashed his press card so quickly Dávid hadn't had a chance to look at it properly. An English press card. Dávid's English was poor at the best of times, worse when he was nervous. For all he knew, the small plastic card could have been a parking pass.

When he thought back on it now, Dávid breathed a sigh of relief that he hadn't let the reporter take his briefcase into the cell room. It rested beside the trash bucket at his feet.

"Only one visitor at a time, eh? Say's who? You?" Nikola braced both arms on the counter and leaned in close, so close Dávid felt the heat of him.

"It's the law--"

"Save your breath. Gimme some paper and a pen, or a pencil, or whatever you use to write with around here." Nikola smirked. "From the looks of you, it could be a crayon."

The implication of the words stung. He'd graduated from the police academy last spring. People should show him more respect. As he passed the paper and pen to Nikola he avoided meeting the man's eyes.

The thug scrawled a few lines on the paper, folded it several times and tossed it on the counter. "Take that to him. Now, not later. I'll be outside. If the visitor doesn't leave in five minutes I'll be back to discuss the problem with you and I'll be pissed off. You can be sure you won't like my personality any better after the discussion."

Dávid fingered the note. Should he read it? How much privacy could a prisoner expect? Why the hell did his superior have to get sick this morning? In the end, curiosity got the better of him and he unfolded the note.

We need to talk. Get rid of your visitor - Nikola

221

Dávid shrugged. Seemed innocent enough. No one had told him Misha couldn't have visitors. He opened the door to the cell room. Two small cells faced each other across a four-foot corridor. Misha sat on the edge of his bed in one cell; the reporter slouched on a chair in the corridor. Both looked up when the door opened.

"A message for you." He passed the note to Misha through the bars.

Several minutes later the reporter retrieved his briefcase and left, grumbling under his breath.

Dávid reached for the phone. Sick or not someone else needed to be here. How could he ask Nikola to empty his pockets before entering the cell room? Impossible. The man would laugh at him as he ignored the request. Then he'd barge through to the cell as if he owned the police station.

As Dávid began to punch in the numbers the door to the police station opened. Nikola smiled as he approached the counter. "Nice work, kid." In one swift movement he grabbed Dávid's shirt, yanked him forward on the counter, jammed a gun under his chin and pulled the trigger.

***

Putyi proved to be a serious, gangly youth with a flush of acne along his hairline. He came armed with an assortment of chess manuals and books, most dog-eared from use. He placed the books on the kitchen table but didn't release his grip on them.

The action was proprietary--you can ask, but don't touch. Stan worked hard to control his laughter before entering into the solemn mood of the moment. With his hands behind his back he paced the kitchen, then stopped in front of Putyi. "Alekhine and Euwe, The Hague,

1937."

Before János could translate the boy reached for a book and flipped through several sections. Names were the same in any language. When Putyi found what he wanted he glanced at Stan and nodded.

"Final move of the game where Alekhine became the first man in history to regain the World Chess Champion title."

This time Putyi turned to János and frowned. The forester translated the request and the boy flipped through the section, finally stopping at a diagram with the moves used in the game listed down the side. Lost for a moment in the world of chess, he smiled as he drew the book closer to his nose and examined the famous moves.

Stan cleared his throat, bringing Putyi back to the present. He eased the book slightly to the side so Stan could read it while he peered over the boy's shoulder. "Black's queen captures white's pawn on the a3 square."

Stan made a quick sketch of the page then thanked the boy. Putyi left as solemnly as he had arrived, clutching his precious books.

As Aunt Anna heated water for coffee Stan returned to his seat at the large kitchen table. The search now belonged to all of them. There was no use keeping his ideas to himself. He traced the edge of his sketch with a thumbnail as he reiterated what he knew about McCartney.

"He collected information during the war that will, even today, be embarrassing to certain interests. Supposedly, he hid that information somewhere on or around the estate. We know he was an avid chess player, and he seems to have left a clue by way of a chess move."

"I wonder why McCartney would need a diagram to remind him where he hid the papers," Sonja said. "I agree that it is probably a clue, but he could have taken the page to give to someone. That person could have come back to get the papers. For all we know, they may already be gone."

Feri raised his cup in the direction of the diagram. "But we agree this page is a clue for where the papers are--or were--located. He's directing us to a move on a chessboard. Where is the board?"

"That I can help with." All eyes turned to János. "Your chessboard, it is perhaps the black and white tiles of swimming pool at chateau."

Stan's pulse kicked into high gear. It made complete sense. If Carl McCartney thought the pool tiles represented a chessboard he would have been drawn to use them as a hiding place. "We need to have a look at that pool."

"Easy enough. Chateau is only two kilometres away. When village people worked there they ride bikes, but we can walk."

"Better yet, we'll drive," Feri stated. "The five of us can fit in the Skoda without the car seat. Eva should stay with Aunt Anna, anyway."

CHAPTER FORTY

Stan's high spirits floundered when he stood on the edge of the chateau's crumbling swimming pool. The foundation was shaped like an enormous letter "D" with the shallow end located in the curve. It gradually deepened as it lengthened toward the straight wall. The pool's floor and walls were lined with large black and white tiles, but if these tiles represented the chessboard in McCartney's clue, which square corresponded to square a1?

To make matters worse, many of the tiles were either missing or broken. As Sonja had suggested, someone may have already found the documents, by chance as much as by design.

Panna circled the edge to the deep end. "This is the only straight wall. Perhaps there are enough tiles for a chess board here?" A gust of chill wind swirled the heap of leaves at the bottom of the pool, rattling the debris with a sound like dry bones.

"Sorry, but that won't work, Panna" Stan replied. "A chess board needs to have eight tiles across and eight tiles down. And the last tile on either side is white. A chessboard has a black tile with a white tile below that, then a black tile--so this doesn't form the same pattern as a chessboard. It was a good idea, but I don't think this is our chess board."

He turned and examined the area around the pool. In its day the pool would have been a pleasant place to spend an afternoon. A row of small cabins sat off to the side behind an overgrown hedge. A place for the guests to change out of their wet bathing suits, perhaps. How many secret meetings of lovers, or spies, were held in those cabins?

The pool deck was large enough to have held tables for afternoon tea and lounge chairs for sunbathing. Stone benches spaced around the perimeter would have provided a place for guests to sit. He selected one in a sunny location and focussed on the chateau, searching for anything in the architecture that resembled a chessboard. The answer was right here, somewhere. He just had to look harder.

Even in its ruined state the building had once been magnificent -- part fort, part hunting lodge, part mansion. He could see where the Karolyi family had added additional wings and ornamentation as their fortunes grew. On the north side, several massive beeches provided a gathering point for a flock of migrating rose-coloured starlings. Suddenly the birds took flight. Something had startled them. A deer, perhaps. Maybe a wild boar.

János joined him. "Karolyi family wealthiest in country. They were social elite. Back then such fancy parties, great hunting parties." He grinned. "Yes, the stories I could tell! Sometimes all-night card games. Then family estates changed hands. Many times they ended in bloody duels."

Near the changing cabins Panna and Sonja shared a bench and giggled like schoolgirls as they acted the part of haughty society ladies lounging at the pool. Feri dutifully played the role of their waiter, serving imaginary cocktails as he egged them on. From the way his jacket hung, Stan realized his brother-in-law had the Makarov in the pocket. Was he expecting trouble?

"I couldn't possibly swim, my dear," Sonja drawled. "I'd get my suit wet." She declined an imaginary drink.

János watched the scene with apparent good humour,

226

then sucked in his breath. He grabbed Stan's arm. "Come!" With no explanation, he pulled Stan toward the changing rooms.

Black and white blocks matching those that lined the pool formed the path in front of the buildings. "The blocks are only two wide. This isn't our chess board," Stan noted. János ignored the remark and pulled at the door of the first room. Over the years the foundation had shifted slightly and made it difficult to open. János pulled again while Stan applied his weight to the frame straightening it enough to free the door.

Sunlight penetrated the room through several holes in the ceiling. Large chunks of missing plaster revealed the lathes in the walls. A concrete bench, similar to the ones at the pool, stood beneath a narrow window set high on the wall. Several clothes hooks studded the wall beneath the window. But it was the floor that caught Stan's attention. Eight rows of alternating black and white squares covered the floor from end to end in either direction. A perfect square. Stan's heart skipped a beat. It looked like they had found their chessboard.

"Are all the rooms the same, Uncle János? Do they all have the same type of floor?"

The forester nodded.

They had found not one but six chessboards Stan realized.

Sonja and Panna tumbled into the small room still laughing. They sobered when they saw the floor. "Oh, Stan," Sonja whispered. "You've found it!"

"Well, maybe. Let's not open any champagne yet. The other five rooms are identical to this one."

"Still, it's only a matter of lifting one tile in each room. Which tile is it?"

Stan removed the drawing from the back pocket of

227

his jeans. "The final move was black's queen capturing white's pawn on the a3 square. That's the first black square on the third row."

"That one!" Panna pointed to the first black square on the third row from the door.

"Or, it could be this one," Feri stated from his spot on the bench under the clothes hooks. McCartney could have viewed the floor as a chess board from this side of the room."

"So, two squares we lift," János said as he unsheathed the hunting knife from his belt and passed it to Stan.

Stan accepted the knife and knelt beside the square. Taking a deep breath he scratched away the loose mortar - - there wasn't much. Over the years the elements had taken their toll. He lifted the tile. Nothing but the concrete base of the cabin.

"Try here!" Feri pointed to his tile with the toe of his shoe.

Again, Stan knelt with the knife. The mortar was missing around the tile and he simply picked it up. Only concrete.

They moved from cabin to cabin. In some, most of the tiles were missing, in others, a sound roof and walls had helped preserve the floor. By the time they reached the fifth cabin Stan's adrenaline was racing. He jammed the knife under the third tile from the door and pried it loose. Instead of concrete, he found dirt.

"Carl McCartney, you bugger, I'd say this is checkmate!" Buried beneath a thin layer of dirt lay a packet wrapped in what may have been oiled canvas.

Around him he registered deep inhales of breathe as he withdrew the package from the cavity that had held it for so many years. As he laid it on the floor a disquieting stench of decay wafted upwards. He glanced at Sonja. "I don't like the smell of this," he murmured.

With trembling fingers he gently peeled back the wrapper. To his horror, as the canvas separated the paper beneath the folds fell apart.

Beside him, Sonja sucked in her breath at the sight of the mouldy contents. "Oh Stan. It's all ruined." János, Feri and Panna crowded closer, jockeying for a better view.

Stan lifted the package from the floor to examine it more closely. Over the years ground water had worked its way into the excavation under the tile; insects, rot and time had taken care of the rest. The result was a stinking swollen mass of rotted paper. A sense of relief overcame him. The powers in Britain who had been so concerned about the reputation of their government during the Second World War, and their monarchy, had nothing to worry about.

"May I see it?" Panna asked as she reached for the package. "I am curious."

Stan was about to hand it to her when a thought struck him. Despite the visible decaying layer, the bundle felt firm, heavy in his hands. If it had rotted completely would it still be so firm? "Just a minute," he said to his sister-in-law. He removed a layer of damaged paper. More oiled canvas. He had it now. McCartney must have doubled wrapped the bundle, to protect it from the elements. No slouch, that man. The second layer of canvas fell away.

Panna hovered beside him. Sonja's breath fluttered against his ear. More paper--this time the writing legible. Then a small notebook, a picture of several men, a slim metal cylinder....

János swore as he pointed to the man on the right in

the photo. "Bastard!" He turned to spit on the floor.

"Well, isn't this an interesting state of affairs." The words came from the doorway. Allan Howland leaned against the frame.

CHAPTER FORTY-ONE

Even from a distance the reek of booze hung about the reporter like a fog. Bleary eyes met Stan's stare from under a fringe of unkempt hair. The man must have pulled an all-night bender.

"*You*! I told you--"

Howland swayed, then grabbed the door frame for support. "Oh yes, you told me all right. But who the hell are you to tell *me* what I can or can't write about? Hmmmm? Got an answer for that, mister big shot RCMP officer?"

"Mr. Howland, you are very drunk." Sonja stepped between Stan and the reporter.

While she blocked the reporter's view Stan quickly rewrapped the package, making sure to replace the rotted portions to conceal the second layer of oiled canvas.

"Of course I'm drunk, madam. That man," he gestured vaguely in Stan's direction, "stole a Pulitzer prize from me. I promised my paper a story of spies, an' looted war treasure, an' conspiracies against the British government. Enough to maybe bring down the monarchy. Wha'd I get? Some low-life gun-runner that the local police can't keep in jail."

It took Stan a moment to process the information. "Misha escaped custody?"

"Yah. He's gone. But he didn't escape. UN put him in a tin-can cell in his own village 'cause they picked him up in Hungary--not in Slovakia."

"Come on, man. Talk sense. If he didn't escape, what happened?"

"Someone came in and got him, thas' what. Walked in and blew the fuckin' head off the kid on duty. Can't

231

tell me that wasn't planned -- young guy like that left on his own to guard a prisoner. Whoever did it, unlocked the cell and walked Misha out the door, I guess. I don't know. Hell, ask the old woman who came to give him his breakfast. She probably knows more about it then I do."

Panna's gasp filled the small room. "Eva! We left Eva with Aunt Anna. Feri, he'll come after you and Stan. He'll find Eva. I'm going back to the house." She pushed past the reporter and hurried down the path.

János followed her out. "I will go, too. In case there is trouble."

When Feri moved toward the door to follow, Allan shot a hand to stop him. "Your kid's okay. Misha won't look for you there."

"Don't play games with me, Howland. If my daughter is in danger--"

"I told you. He won't go to Aunt Anna's... or whatever her name is." He shook his shaggy head. "This morning -- real early, went to interview 'im. He asked about you guys. You know, Boyko, you pissed me off real good. An' I'd had a few drinks last night."

Stan held up the packet of McCartney's papers. "So you told him about the papers, and the chateau."

"You got it." He tried a wink but couldn't pull it off. "We started talking about you, about the chateau. All that crap. Then the police guard.... A *kid*. How could someone do that to him? He was just a *kid*."

Allan's face softened with pity for a moment. Stan understood the emotion. He'd seen his share of people dying for being at the wrong place at the wrong time, or because they simply stood for an unpopular idea.

"Anyway, the guard came in with a note. Misha, he read it, 'an asked me to go get him a change of clothes. Said his wife didn't want to come see him in a jail cell, would I go get them from her." Howland scowled. "I'm an ass, I believed him. When I got to the hotel his wife didn't know what I was talking about." He giggled, then tried to cover his mouth with his hand.

"You ask me, the old girl seemed happy to hear where he was. But I knew something was up, so I went back to what passes for a jail in that hick-town. From on the street I could hear the woman who brought breakfast-- screaming."

Horror filled his eyes as he recalled the scene. Sonja groped for Stan's arm. When he glanced at her he saw the same horror reflected in hers.

Howland continued his story, his voice pitched so low they strained to hear him. "Guess she'd brought Misha his breakfast...pancakes, eggs. The stuff littered the floor where she'd dropped it. That poor kid, his body draped over the counter. The door to the cell room stood open and Misha...pffft." Allan spread his fingers. "Gone. The place looked like a Goddamned wild west movie."

"I'm not surprised," Feri said. "Disappointed, but not surprised. Sipos couldn't trust Misha to keep his mouth shut."

"So, why didn't he just kill him?" Sonja asked.

She had a good point. Why not shoot Misha in the jail cell? It would send a message to the others that they'd better keep their mouths shut, no matter how little they knew about the operation. One answer made sense -- Sipos had sprung Misha because he needed him.

For whatever reason Misha was loose, Stan agreed with Howland's assumption--Misha would steer clear of the Telke's house. Everyone in the district knew him. Now he was more than a fugitive, he was an accessory to murder. The people around him may put up with a bit of smuggling, but not with murder. Especially since the kid was a local, and a police officer. Chances were Misha would head to Budapest where Sipos could get him out of the country. Somewhere that didn't have an extradition agreement with Hungary--either Turkey or Egypt.

"Oh, my goddamned knees," Allan pushed away from the doorframe and made his way across the room to the bench. "Let's get back to those papers. I can offer you big money for them and whatever else is in that package. There's also something called freedom of the press. People have a right to know what went on during the war years. Ya' know what I mean?"

"Sorry, Howland. I'm not interested. And even if I was, the material is useless." Stan turned to leave the change room. "Come on." He gestured to Feri and Sonja. "We're done here."

"Useless? Aww, come on. I wasn't born yesterday. The Hitler diaries sold for $4,000,000.00, and they were *fake*! You might want to reconsider my offer. Newspaper men have their sources. I've made it my business to learn the charming history of your sweet little family."

The reporter's words stopped Stan cold. He turned. "Care to explain that comment?"

"For starters, I know all about Feri's former employer. And who knows? Maybe he still works for Sipos. I wonder what CSIS would make of something like that. One of their officers with a gangster for a brother-in-law. Then, there's your wife."

Stan's annoyance gave way to anger. "You bastard." He shoved the package at Feri. It may not accomplish much to beat the crap out of Howland, but it sure would feel good. He balled his fists and took a step toward the reporter.

Sonja grabbed his shirt. "No, Stan. Please, don't.

234

He's drunk. Let's just leave."

Howland struggled to his feet. Whether it was the liquor or his knees that betrayed him, Stan realized the man could barely stand. There would be no satisfaction in attacking him. His fists dropped.

"Doesn't sound great, does it, cop? I can guarantee it won't look any prettier in print. Little woman sold by her brother. Sent to Canada as a sex slave--" His eyes widened in amazement at something he saw over Stan's shoulder.

As Stan turned, Sonja gasped. Misha had slipped unnoticed into the room. He held her in a chokehold. In his other hand he held a gun, pointed at her ribs.

"If everyone stays calm she won't get hurt. Feri, I want you to hand that package to your sister."

Stan held his hands up, palms out. "Let her go first. Nothing happens until you let her go."

"You're not in a position to bargain. I'll need her and the Mercedes out there to leave the district. Whatever is in that package will make up for the fat profit you cost me on the arms deal."

A movement in his peripheral vision caught Stan's attention. Feri. He was going to give Misha McCartney's papers.

Howland sagged onto the bench. "And us?" he whispered.

Misha angled his weapon toward the reporter. "Well, big shot, let's just say you won't be needing your car anymore."

CHAPTER FORTY-TWO

Feri stepped forward with the Makarov in his hand, not the papers.

A shot exploded in the small room, followed by a softer echo. Allan Howland grunted, then toppled from the bench. Misha fell to the ground without a sound. Feri dropped his gun and wrapped his arms around his sister.

"I couldn't let you down again, Sonja. Not a second time." He turned her away from the body on the floor. McCartney's papers lay abandoned at their feet.

Stan shoved Allan's howls of pain to the back of his mind as he squatted beside Misha. No pulse. Unlike the reporter, Misha was dead. Shot through the back. Stan reached for Feri's gun and sniffed the barrel. The weapon hadn't been fired. He shoved the piece across the floor in Feri's direction and grabbed Misha's fallen gun.

"Away from the door! Shooter outside!"

Feri yanked Sonja into a corner as Stan rolled to the edge of the room. He grasped Howland by his coat collar and tugged him out of the line of fire. The reporter bellowed in pain.

Another shot struck the wall above the bench drawing a gasp from Sonja.

Stan crabwalked to the corner where Feri and Sonja crouched. "Whoever it is, he knows Misha's down. He's after someone else. I'll give you three guesses who's behind this."

"I only need one," Feri replied. "Sipos. He found out who put the smuggling ring out of business and he wants revenge. What do you think, Allan? Any idea who might have given Sipos the information?"

The reporter whimpered. "I'm bleeding to death.

Help me." Blood oozed through his fingers where he grasped his thigh.

Stan glanced at Allan's wounded leg. An area of his pants above the knee glistened red with blood, but none pooled on the floor. The bullet hadn't struck an artery. "You'll live. Be happy that slug in his back interfered with Misha's aim.

"We need to call János," Stan said. He dug his cell from his pocket and tossed it to Feri. "Tell him we need the police and an ambulance. And ask him to get over here with that old shotgun of his, but not to come near the pool area. Just shoot into the air from the driveway. It should be enough to make whoever the hell it is out there decide to clear out."

He turned to Sonja. In the dim light her face seemed deathly pale. "You okay?"

She nodded as she slid to the floor, her back in the corner. "Just faint...a little faint... Feri didn't shoot Misha did he? Tell me he didn't."

Light-headedness Stan could take, as long as she wasn't hurt. "Don't worry. He didn't."

"Only because someone did it first," Feri stated. "Like I said--I wouldn't have let you down again."

Several feet to the right of Sonja's head a hole in the cabin wall allowed Stan a partial view of the checkerboard pathway and a corner of the pool. No one moved in his sight line. The shooter could have fired from behind any number of shrubs or trees. By now he could have worked his way behind the change room.

Stan fired a shot through the door but received no answering fire. Fair enough. At least the killer knew they had a weapon and were willing to use it. It would be too much to hope he had left; content in knowing Misha was dead. More likely he thought he had them pinned down and could wait them out. At some point they would have to leave the building. Thank God for cell phones.

Feri finished the call and snapped the phone shut. "He's on his way. I hope he follows your instructions and stays out of the line of fire. He's a pretty headstrong old man. What do you think Stan -- this would explain why Misha left his jail cell alive. Whoever arranged for his escape used him to track us down."

Allan wiped a bloody hand on his pant leg. "Oh God, so much blood. You wouldn't happen to have a drink on you?" His eyes darted to the body on the floor. "Even...water?"

His words roused Sonja. She scooted across the floor on her butt. "We should put some pressure on that leg. Maybe use part of your shirt for a bandage. Stan, what did you do with Uncle János knife?"

"It's on the other side of the bench. Nobody exposes themselves in the doorway to get it. Tear the shirt, use the whole thing, I don't care. But stay put."

A shot smacked into the exterior of the far wall. The impact loosened the crumbling stucco enough for a chunk to fall away. A hole the size of a fist appeared between the lathes, a coat of fine powder settled on the floor amid the other debris. With enough time and ammunition, the shooter would turn the change hut into Swiss cheese. From there it would be a matter of picking them off, one by one.

Stan sent a round back through the hole. Brush thrashed and snapped on the other side. He'd bought a few valuable minutes.

He turned his attention to the reporter. Allan grimaced as he worked himself out of his shirt. From experience Stan knew every move hurt like hell. It was probably a flesh wound, but still, he should check it out.

He hunkered down beside the man and helped rip his shirt.

"You know, Howland, you brought this mess on us and yourself. If you'd listened to me in the first place you would have given up on the papers. Sipos wouldn't have become involved and Misha wouldn't have shown up here today."

Other than a grunt, Allan made no comment.

Stan tore the pant leg open, examined the wound, and placed a pad of wadded shirt over the area. As he'd suspected, the wound wouldn't kill him, although the bullet had ploughed a nasty furrow. He bound the pad in place with the shirt's sleeve.

"And you've got your exclusive on the smugglers. If we live you'll have a lot to celebrate. But you'll sure as hell have a hard time explaining how a gangster and a woman in the sex trade ended up saving your sorry ass." Stan gave the bandage a final tug.

Howland's eyes bulged but he managed to remain silent.

"Sorry about that, but I wanted to get your attention," Stan snapped. He scooped the package from the floor and lifted a corner of the rotten canvas to reveal the mass of pulp beneath. "This is what might get us killed. Like I said, it's worthless. You should have done yourself a favour. Been happy with the story you had."

Allan eyed the packet of papers. "I'm a reporter, dammit! It's my training, what I'm paid to do."

"Does that training include blackmail? Threats? Associating with people like Sipos? Look where it's brought you. Where it's brought all of us. Selling your soul to the devil makes for good fiction, Allan, but that's where it should stay. We're in the real world here and I don't care much that my wife is paying for your

239

ambition."

CHAPTER FORTY-THREE

Another shot tore away a substantial chunk of wall. Stan checked his watch. Six minutes since the phone call to János. Radvany was two kilometres from the chateau over hard-packed gravel. János wouldn't waste time along the way. He should be on the estate by now.

Feri's thoughts moved along the same ground. "If János comes up the main drive he could end up between the shooter and the guy's vehicle. Not good."

"The old man's pretty cagey. A place like this will have access roads for deliveries and services -- garbage collection -- that kind of thing. He worked on the estate so he knows where they are, or where they were. They'd still be passable on foot."

He glanced at Sonja. Her lips set in a firm line, she fussed over Allan's bandage. Given that Howland had just threatened to dish up the sordid details of her past in the press, he was lucky she paid attention to his plight at all.

Stan inched closer to Feri and lowered his voice to a whisper. "We can't depend on the police. I agree with Howland -- the local cops were paid to let Misha operate under their radar. They'll need to cover their asses after what happened in the town. Misha escaping like that...folks will be asking a lot of questions. I don't expect they'll break any speed records getting out here for our benefit."

The throaty sound of a shotgun blast rumbled through the clear air. Not near at hand, but close enough to act as a signal. Stan smiled as he slid along the wall toward the door. "Our white knight has arrived. Feri, how about you tell our friend out there we've called in reinforcements. It

241

might help him decide it's time to leave. Just don't tell him our saviour is one old gentleman with an antique shotgun."

"*Figyelj rám!*" Listen up, Feri shouted. Several sentences followed with no response from their attacker. After a short pause he tried again. This time they heard a curse and the rustle of dry shrubbery.

He'd got the message. Or perhaps a last-minute ruse to flush them out? The shotgun blasted again, this time near the chateau. Footsteps whispered across the tiles on the walkway. He hadn't left, but he was on the move.

Stan angled for a view through the door. The figure of a man disappeared behind the cabana closest to the pool and the chateau. *What the hell?* The shooter wasn't moving away from János, but toward the sound of gunfire. Once the old man cleared the corner of the building he would be an easy target.

Stan eased out of the cabin doorway followed closely by Feri. With a hand motion Stan directed his brother-in-law to move along the hedgerow, still full enough with crimson leaves to offer good concealment.

The back of the change buildings was a tangle of dead vegetation. Ankle-gripping vines slowed Stan's pace. He hugged the walls, travelling as silently as possible through the pungent leaf litter. The lay-out of the estate was a mystery to him. In their eagerness to see the pool when they arrived they had walked directly from the parking lot to the back of the chateau. He regretted that now. He had no idea where the shooter could find cover.

The gunman hadn't made a break for it when he had the chance. Did he want to see who Stan had called for help and report that information back to Sipos? Even if he got a good look at János he wouldn't know who the man was...unless...yes, of course! The shooter had to be local. Sipos wouldn't have had enough time to send someone from Budapest to take care of the problem.

Feri had mentioned enough about his former boss for Stan to have a good idea about the man's black moods. Sipos' mind was like a steel trap when it came to business, but once angered he exploded in a fury that bordered on madness. His actions defied all attempts at reason, sometimes for days. Now, with his business in this part of Hungary in a shambles, the crime lord would be in a murderous rage. Thanks to Allan Howland, Sipos knew the names of everyone who had a hand in destroying that business.

If Stan's assessment was on the mark, Sipos would want everyone involved in his misfortune eliminated--not just Stan and Feri, but possibly János and Sonja as well. Another thought struck him. Allan knew the connection between Sipos and Misha. He might be on a hit list. Allan and Sonja were unprotected in the cabana.

Stan rounded the corner of the first hut. Other than Feri crouched by the hedge, the area was empty. It shouldn't take this long for János to make it around the main building to the pool.

Stan raised his arm to motion Feri back to the cabana when the shotgun thundered for the third time--close at hand.

Feri pointed to a service shed set back from the corner of the main house. He silently mouthed the words: "Over there."

The long expanse of pool deck offered no cover to approach the sagging building. They'd have to circle around the chateau. It would take time. Precious time.

As Stan contemplated his next move Uncle János stepped out from behind the shed. "I thought it is wild boar that stalks me from bush, so I shoot. Now I see it is man."

A body lay in an overgrown tangle of hawthorn and lilac shrubs behind the shed. Stan patted pockets and extracted a wallet and cell phone. A driver's license put a name to the killer: Nikola Kosma from Ujhely.

"I remember him. He came to visit Sipos a couple of times," Feri stated.

Stan turned his attention to the cell phone, a cheap model that thugs around North America bought for illegal use and then tossed. Their counterparts in Europe would be doing the same thing. He had little doubt who had been the last caller on the phone. He pressed the redial button. Two rings later the call connected, but no one spoke on the other end.

"Give it up, Sipos. It didn't work," Stan said. "Nikola's dead." Before he could continue the listener disconnected the call.

Stan pocketed the phone. He'd turn it over to the local police, but he put no stock in them being able to trace any of the calls. Sipos would have used a disposable phone as well.

***

"How long before the ambulance gets here?" Allan punctuated his query with a grimace. "I'm practically a dead man. Look at this *blood*!"

Stan patted the reporter on the shoulder as he rose. The bandage seemed to have stopped the bleeding. "I'll check with Feri."

"No. Don't leave me alone in here. Not with that...that thing! That body. Boyko come back! *Please*."

Stan grinned as he followed the black and white tiled

path from the cabana back to the pool deck. Sonja sat on one of the stone benches, Feri beside her. Uncle János stood guard over the body of the assassin behind the shed.

"I think our Mr. Howland is dissatisfied with the condition of his change room, Stan said as he joined them. "Have you called Panna?"

"Yes, everything is fine there." Feri handed Stan his cell phone. "They've called the police--again--and an ambulance is on the way. It shouldn't be long. I think they should check Sonja, too. She's very light-headed and she chucked up her breakfast."

Stan crouched at her feet. He took her hands in his. "Sonja?"

She squeezed his hands gently before drawing hers away. "Oh don't be silly, you guys. I'm just relieved I won't have to tell our child his, or maybe her, father was shot while we were on vacation in Hungary."

Sonja patted her belly and laughed in delight at the startled look on Stan's face.

***

Sipos kneaded the tense muscles at the back of his neck. He had to calm down. Had to. He made mistakes when he lost control. First things first--ditch the phone. No big loss there. There were a dozen more just like it in the warehouse. Later, when things settled down, he'd deal with the cop, and with Sonja. Canada wasn't so far away these days.

CHAPTER FORTY-FOUR

Stan acknowledged the ambassador's wave.

He'd been doing that a lot lately--waving. He'd waved good-bye to Uncle János and Aunt Anna yesterday. Today he'd waved good-bye to little Eva. The child had clung to him like an octopus, arms and legs wound around him tightly. How old would she be when he saw her again? Maybe, if things worked out for Feri and Panna, the family could come to Canada for a visit. That would be nice.

"I'll just be a moment," he told Sonja as he directed her to the edge of the reception hall. "Do you mind visiting with Feri and Panna for a bit?"

"Of course not. I want to get Aunt Anna's mailing address, anyway."

Stan threaded his way through the crowded room.

Allan Howland held court in one corner, the Ambassador's secretary, Jordan Hastings, dancing attendance. His arrival on crutches had created a stir. When Stan overheard the reporter's version of the events that led to his condition Stan had difficulty suppressing a chuckle. *Must be what they call creative license.* One statement was true, however--the reporter would be wise to leave Hungary. Thankfully, he hadn't mentioned Uncle János' name to Sipos.

Ambassador Graham extended his hand. "Good evening. I trust you're enjoying this little get together?"

"Totally unnecessary, but appreciated. It's nice to have a chance to say goodbye before we leave tomorrow."

"Back to Winnipeg?"

"No. We're off to Greece. It will be a while before we'll have a chance to come back to Europe." He paused.

246

The words still seemed foreign on his tongue. "My wife and I will be busy raising a family for the next few years."

Walter Graham smiled, an action that transformed his stern features. "Congratulations. You'll have much to remember Hungary for in the future. It's also my pleasure to tell you I've sent a commendation by diplomatic pouch to be inserted in your file. Given the nature of your assignment, I'm afraid it can't be made public."

Stan tried to hide his flush of pleasure. "I understand. I spent some time with the British ambassador a little earlier. They're appreciative."

In fact, Stan reflected, Roger Avery, the Queen's representative in Hungary, had been more than appreciative. How did the old saying go? Knowledge is power. Even if that knowledge embarrasses your own government. Given the advances in forensic technology, the British government could probably make all the documents legible, even those that were damaged.

"It's too bad you got dragged into that nasty business in Fuzer. While I had Ottawa on the line today we had a little chat about it."

Stan accepted a glass of wine from a hostess. "Anything further on Sipos Sandor?" Sipos' fate weighed heavy on Stan. The man had sold Sonja into prostitution as punishment for defying him. That she had managed to extricate herself from his plans must gall him. Add to that, anger for Stan's role in breaking up the smuggling ring--well, Sipos had even more reason to hate both of them.

"Afraid not. Sipos is like Teflon--nothing sticks to him. Since Misha Kormos is dead, there's no evidence to link Sipos with the guns. Misha's cell phone has disappeared from the evidence room in Szephalom. It would be interesting to know who has it--and what they

247

extracted from it."

Disappointing news, but Stan wasn't surprised. The police officer in charge at the station would need something to bankroll his future once he was dismissed. *If* he was dismissed. The corruption may go further than the local police unit. Stan was glad several thousand miles separated Hungary from Canada and his family.

He sipped the wine; deep red with a taste of cherries and spice. He'd had it before. This was the same wine he had ordered at the sidewalk café when Sonja recognized Sipos on the street. "Egri Bikavér?" Stan asked as he raised his glass to examine the contents.

"Bull's blood." Sonja laughed as she joined them. She slipped her arm through his. "I'm afraid your Hungarian hasn't improved at all. But not to worry. In a few months you'll be learning a new language made up entirely of one syllable words."

Ambassador Graham chuckled. "May we get you a coffee, or perhaps a soft drink?"

She shook her head. "Thank you, but Feri and Panna need to leave."

Stan extended his hand to the ambassador. "That means it's time for us to say good-night, and good-bye, as well."

He escorted her across the floor to where Feri and Panna waited. The couple would be leaving Budapest with Eva early in the morning. Feri had assured them he and Panna were quite content to manage her uncle's antique shop in Holloko. The old man had even given them an option to buy the business in the future.

"Holloko is a better place to raise children," Panna said yesterday as she cuddled her daughter. "These things become important. You will see."

Stan could concede part of her reasoning. Budapest

was a fascinating city to visit but he could not envision raising his children here. For the other part--his sister-in-law had avoided the real issue. The threat of Sipos' retaliation had precipitated their move, not the offer of the business in Holloko, or the challenges of raising a child in a fast-paced city. Sipos controlled their lives even as he remained a free man. At some point, he would slip up and be put away. Stan wished he could be there when it happened.

He set the thoughts aside. Greece with its beaches and ancient ruins beckoned. A true holiday this time--no searching for missing relatives or buried treasure. His arm stole around Sonja's waist. No fear of attack by a gangster bent on settling a score.

Sonja leaned closer and whispered in his ear, her voice husky, "Tonight, you and I, we should say good-bye to Hungary."

***

Sipos listened to the recorded music while he waited for someone to come on the line.

Finally: "Malév Hungarian Airlines. How may I help you?"

"Yes. Tell me, please, what is required to visit Winnipeg? In Canada. I'm not travelling immediately, but I like to plan in advance."

THE END